Iltudus Th

How to Manage it

Vol. 3

SALZWASSER
VERLAG

Iltudus Thomas Prichard

How to Manage it

Vol. 3

Reprint of the original, first published in 1864.

1st Edition 2022 | ISBN: 978-3-75259-404-1

Verlag (Publisher): Salzwasser Verlag GmbH, Zeilweg 44, 60439 Frankfurt, Deutschland
Vertretungsberechtigt (Authorized to represent): E. Roepke, Zeilweg 44, 60439 Frankfurt, Deutschland
Druck (Print): Books on Demand GmbH, In de Tarpen 42, 22848 Norderstedt, Deutschland

HOW TO MANAGE IT.

VOL. III.

HOW TO MANAGE IT:

A NOVEL.

BY

ILTUDUS THOMAS PRICHARD

(LATE BENGAL ARMY).

'Quæque ipse miserrima vidi.'

IN THREE VOLUMES.

VOL. III.

LONDON:

1864.

HOW TO MANAGE IT.

CHAPTER XLI.

For the next ten days such was the state of constant alarm in which the residents at Aurungabad remained that life became almost unendurable. Not a single day, scarcely an hour, passed without some alarming report being spread of the approach of a large body of insurgents, who would sack the place, burn down the houses, and certainly murder every luckless European or Christian that fell into their hands. On these occasions all the non-combatants, that is, the women and children—for every man in those days, whatever his cloth or profession, was a combatant—betook themselves in a hurried helter-skelter way to the fort, remained there till the panic had subsided or been proved groundless, and then returned to their houses. The practical result of this was, that people were constantly on the move, the women to the fort, and the men to the parade-ground or the place of rendezvous; and seeing that the weather was excessively hot, that it was the season during which exposure to the sun is always avoided as much as possible by people who have any regard for their constitution, it became excessively irksome.

Aurungabad was just on the high road to the imperial city, now the focus of insurrection. Almost every body of mutineers, from however distant a station, had to pass by or near Aurungabad on their way to Delhi. That it had not been attacked twenty times over within as many days after the first outbreak was most marvellous, and only to be explained by the unaccountable manner in which the mutineers conducted all their proceedings from the very first. They never did anything at the right time, nor put anything in the right place. They carried on their operations by fits and starts, setting everybody's calculations out, and filling with surprise those who watched the eccentric progress of the rebellion. Sooner or later, however, it seemed certain that Aurungabad would be attacked by a powerful body of mutineers, who would probably be joined by the city people, and then the position of the residents could not fail to be most precarious. With so small a body of men as they had, it was quite impossible to protect every place and everybody. Divided into small detachments and scattered about over the station, the soldiers would become an easy prey, and the force be cut up in detail. On the other hand, if the brigade was collected at any one given place, there were so many assailable points and posts urgently requiring protection within a circuit of fifteen or twenty miles, that the greatest possible mischief might be done at one spot, while the troops were operating at another perhaps five miles off.

It is not to be wondered at that many a wistful gaze was turned to the fort, and many a proposition whispered round to abandon the two stations and let everyone take up his abode inside the fort, which was large enough to hold all the residents, with a good deal of cramming. This expedient was rendered still more advisable, if not necessary, by the laudable energy of the civilians, who in a most praiseworthy manner set to work to repair the damage that had been done by the defection of the troops, and began, the morning following the mutiny, to raise another police force to replace that which was gone. Enlisting went on daily in the compound of Mr. Octavius Cæsar Simple, C. S., Inspector-General of

Police in the central provinces; and it was an argument frequently brought forward by that gentleman and his official associates, of the depth to which the spirit of affection and loyalty towards our government had taken root in the minds of the people, notwithstanding a few indications to the contrary, that the lower orders flocked in crowds to be enlisted in the new police battalions.

It is true a bounty of three rupees was given to each man that came forward, but this was only to stimulate them to exertion, and not with any view to kindling a spirit of loyalty which did not exist before.

By some strange fatality, and very much to the astonishment of Mr. Simple and his brother civilians, the very day the new battalion was complete, the men mutinied, cut off Mr. Simple's head, and after parading it about the place stuck it on one of the gate-posts of Government House, and then proceeded to plunder houses and set fire to them, and murder a few pensioners' families who had escaped the last massacre, and behave in what the Honourable George Gregory's secretary described in his report on the occurrence, 'a very irregular manner.'

The marauders were cut short in their work by the uncovenanted cavalry, who had now formed themselves into a separate body, composed exclusively of men belonging to that class who served the government without being under a covenant. They sabred a few of the most daring, and drove the rest out of the place. Whether they came back again or not was never known, but the Honourable George Gregory, who had received his political education in a school which taught that lessons derived from experience were not worth learning, the day following the mutiny of the second police battalion issued orders for immediately raising a third. But this time, by the advice of his secretary, he directed that, instead of giving each man a bounty of three rupees, every recruit should be made to pay that sum as a kind of guarantee for his good behaviour. Much to the surprise of several *quidnuncs*, who gravely shook their heads and prognosticated complete failure to a system so entirely void of precedent, so many applicants for service flocked to the new inspector-general of police that, before the third day was out, he had under him a force as large as the former one, every man of whom had paid government three rupees for the honour of enlisting. The Hon. George Gregory pointed triumphantly to this fact in an able minute written about this time to the governor-general as a convincing proof 'that the rebellion was an exclusively military movement, and that disaffection had not spread beyond the ranks of the army.'

It happened at last that Aurungabad was really threatened by a hostile force, variously estimated from a lac to five thousand, mutineers of all arms, who were passing up towards Delhi, and had given out their intention of sacking Aurungabad on the way. Brigadier Littlesole, after communicating with the Prefect, determined to take his brigade out and give them battle before they came very near the station; and accordingly, leaving the place under the protection of the new police, watched by a small detachment of the uncovenanted cavalry, the European brigade marched against the enemy. The spot the brigadier determined to attack them was just twenty miles from Aurungabad.

When they got there they found the mutineers drawn up in a strong position, with some heavy batteries constructed under cover of a grove of trees, from which a galling fire was opened on the brigadier's line as soon as they came within range. The horse artillery lost no time in replying, but the calibre of the enemy's guns was so much greater than ours, that it was impossible for the horse artillery to silence his fire. It was therefore determined to bring up the infantry, and the flank companies of the 159th were moved out in skirmishing order to cover the advance of the line.

On the order 'to load' being given, some hesitation was observed among the men, when the discovery was made that blank ammunition had been served out to them instead of balled.

In fact, except in the pistols of the officers and of the detachment of uncovenanted cavalry who accompanied the force, there was not a bullet in the whole brigade. This was rather awkward; but Brigadier Littlesole was equal to the occasion, and at once ordered a retreat, observing to some of his staff who were riding with him at the time, 'that a retreat in the face of an enemy often proved a commander's ability even more than an advance.' The mutineers seeing this unaccountable move on the part of the English line, and observing moreover that the retreat of the brigade was being conducted in such an orderly and leisurely manner that it could not possibly have originated in anything but a ruse, suddenly became panic-struck, and deserted the field in a most disorderly manner. They even left their guns in position under the trees, undefended.

The gallant commander of the uncovenanted

cavalry ordered his men to charge; they did so, and the result was that they captured all the guns, there being no one to defend them.

Meantime the rest of the brigade was wending its way back to Aurungabad, and the uncovenanted cavalry determined not to lose the prize—and no bad prize either, being two batteries of heavy siege guns with ammunition complete—resolved to remain and protect them till elephants were sent to bring them in. This gallant little body was commanded by a man named Augustus Tupper, who from a habit he had acquired, perhaps purposely assumed, of expressing himself always in proverbial style, was generally supposed to be the brother of the man renowned for his famous literary amalgam of original sentiment and mutilated proverbs of Solomon.

One of the troopers had been sent into cantonments to report the capture of the guns and to bring out elephants to fetch them in, but as he had not returned by midnight, it was determined to spike the guns and leave them, as the troop had no forage for their horses and no food for themselves. They did so, and marched for Aurungabad, reaching the station next morning about nine o'clock. Great was their astonishment to find it deserted, while the crowds of people streaming towards the fort indicated at once the direction the residents had disappeared in. Anxious to find out what was the matter, Tupper set his men into a gallop, and hurried down the road towards the fort-gate. No sooner had they got within range than the guns opened fire, and Tupper's gallant band had one or two empty saddles before they had ridden many yards. There was nothing for it, however, but to ride on. When they came within musket range they had to run the gauntlet of a heavy file firing from the 159th, which did not stop till the remnant of the detachment of uncovenanted cavalry drew rein within easy earshot of the fort-gate. A short parley ensued, and they were admitted inside: then followed mutual explanations, the result of which may be given briefly as follows:—

The news of the retreat of the brigade had spread like wildfire back to Aurungabad, but exaggerated of course into a total rout of the whole force. The remnant, it was said, were making the best of their way back, followed up by the enemy excited with their success. About an hour after this report had got wind in the station, the police battalion who had been left for its protection mutinied, and commenced plundering and burning houses. The civilians' wives and families, panic-struck, fled to the fort; the families in cantonments did the same. All was confusion and trepidation; but by evening so intent were the new police on realising plunder, that all the residents and non-combatants had succeeded in reaching the fort in safety. Towards evening the 159th and artillery came in; but finding the whole place in the possession of the rebel police and rabble from the city who had joined them, being spread in parties of tens and twenties in every house and outhouse in cantonments, it was hopeless attempting to dislodge them that night; so the brigade made straight for the fort.

They passed an uncomfortable night, but before morning intelligence was brought that the mutineers were in full force marching straight on Aurungabad. The approach of Tupper's men was magnified into this. The nearer they came the more alarmed grew the garrison. At last the guns were loaded, and directly the supposed enemy came within range fire was opened.

Search was made for the volunteer who had been sent in for the elephants. After a long time he was found in the commissariat store-house, dead drunk. He had gone there on first arriving to speak to the commissariat officer about the elephants, but an open barrel of spirits which had just before been 'stove in' by a mischievous soldier was too much for him, and he forgot all about Tupper, the guns, and the elephants, and gave himself up to the unrestrained enjoyment of undiluted rum.

Augustus Tupper was put under arrest and tried subsequently for disobedience of orders. Elephants were sent out to bring in the guns, but meantime they had been taken away, and one of the mahouts, or elephant drivers, having seized the opportunity of deserting to the enemy and taking the beast he had charge of with him, a bill for the price of the lost elephant—twelve hundred rupees—and for two days' fodder for the rest, was sent in against the luckless commandant of uncovenanted cavalry, and his pay was mulcted to make good the deficiency. He was deprived of the command of the cavalry, and reduced from the position of head to that of junior clerk to the Board of Red Tape for disobedience of orders.

After these events the residents of Aurungabad by common consent confined themselves in their fort. The panic increased daily, the natives laughed, the European soldiers lost all respect for their superiors, and threw off the restraints of discipline; civilians and military men squabbled about precedence, and their wives took part; an order issued by the civil authorities was counter-ordered by the military, and then issued by the latter to their own subordinates, discussed, and if agreeable or approved of obeyed, if not, disregarded. The Honourable George Gregory died, and finally cholera burst out among the crowded and helpless residents, and made sad havoc in domestic circles.

CHAPTER XLII.

THE intelligence of the abandonment of the station and cantonment of Aurungabad spread like wildfire through the whole of the central provinces. Chiefs and powerful zemindars, who had hitherto wavered in their allegiance, now threw all their influence into the scale against the British government. The people who had no regular employment all set off to join the rebels, or raised the standard of rebellion in their own towns and villages; the old bands of dacoits and professional robbers, who had been hunted down and kept quiet under the firm hand of British rule, suddenly sprang into life and energy, and revelled in the indulgence of their predatory habits. The country was devastated by fire and sword; every man's hand was against his neighbour. The most frightful atrocities were committed. Even unoffending women and children were put to death with the most revolting cruelty, to gratify some cherished spite; the wealthy were impoverished, the low riff-raff became rich and gorged with plunder; in short, all was anarchy and confusion. Under such circumstances, of course, it was impossible for any European to remain in the district. All the out-stations were abandoned, and the residents, planters, railway officials, and every-one with a white face, made the best of their way to the Aurungabad fort, there to wait till the storm had blown over. There could not have been less than four or five thousand fugitives altogether in the fort; of these, about a thousand were soldiers, or men at any rate trained to arms, who had had the advantage of a military education. Of the rest, there were at least six or seven hundred able-bodied fighting men, many of whom had horses and arms; the remainder were non-combatants.

To give any description of the state of confusion that these people were in would be utterly impossible. It can with difficulty be imagined; families accustomed to every luxury were huddled together into quarters which, in former days, they would have thought too wretched for their horses. Delicately nurtured ladies and still more delicate children were forced to live in cramped-up little cells without proper ventilation, deprived of all the appliances for cooling the heated atmosphere by which art has rendered residence in a tropical climate not unendurable. People who had been accustomed to be waited on by hosts of servants, were obliged to attend to their own wants and give themselves up to the merest drudgery, and that, too, with all the disadvantages of the hot weather, insufficient apparatus, and failing health. In short, the artificial distinctions and barriers of society were overturned, and all were reduced to one dead level, the really rich being those who had strong constitutions and unflagging spirits.

For some time after the death of the Honourable George Gregory, confusion was made worse confounded by the disorganisation of the government for want of a constituted head. The Honourable George had been carried off suddenly by an attack of cholera, so that he had died without having left any instruction as to his successor. Meantime the central provinces, after being in insurrection for a fortnight, had by an order of government been put under martial law. This Brigadier Littlesole interpreted to mean that civil government had ceased: he was supported by his staff, and in fact by all the military who held the same opinion. Not so the civil world: they held to the maxim *cedant arma togæ*, and would not allow that any circumstance could establish the converse. So the question was referred to the supreme government at Calcutta, for happily, at that time, communication with the presidency had not been cut off. At the same time that this knotty point was referred to the arbitration of the governor-general and council, they were earnestly solicited to name the successor to the Honourable George with the least possible delay, accompanying the selection with a plain letter of instructions, defining beyond all possibility of cavil the duties of each department, and, of course, of the chief functionaries. Meantime, the supreme government of the central provinces had been assumed by the next senior civilian to the deceased, viz. Quintilian Edward Dormouse, who was very fond of signing his initials on the outside cover of official documents, for the sake, as he said, of enlivening the dreary drudgery of official routine by a little pleasantry.

Party feeling ran high. All the military declared they would only look upon their immediate head as the representative of government. All the civilians and uncovenanted denied the right of any but a civilian to rule; while the independent classes, and they were pretty numerous, laughed at both, and acted as they thought best for themselves. But the really sensible men of all classes regretted extremely this unsettled and disorganised state of things, and were only anxious to see some one individual invested with supreme power, for the sake of putting an end to the disgraceful anarchy that prevailed. The answer from government, however, was very long in coming.

When the late Prefect had taken up his abode in the fort, he had insisted on the quarters he occupied being called Government House. A flag-staff had been erected immediately in front of the door, and a small gun on its carriage kept there, partly for security, partly to add a dignity that the Prefect's quarters did not certainly possess without, and partly for the purpose of firing salutes on certain state occasions. This arrangement had never been interfered with, except that the flag had been hauled down when the Prefect died.

One day the utmost consternation was spread throughout the thickly-populated garrison by the report of cannon in their immediate proximity. The panic was short-lived, for it soon became evident that the firing was a salute, and that it came from the quarters known as Government House. Scarcely had the sixth gun been counted, when a second salute began from the neighbourhood of the brigadier's quarters. All was perplexity, doubt, and anxiety. Had Delhi fallen? Had the Prince of Wales arrived in Calcutta, at the head of an enormous army? Had the governor-general himself reached Aurungabad? These and such like questions flew from mouth to mouth; but no one could answer them. By-and-by it became noised abroad that a meeting had been called at the armoury, which was the largest building available for public purposes in the fort, and thither pressed an eager crowd in spite of hot winds and a burning sun, for it was given out that here they would receive a solution of the mystery of the double salute. To this meeting I must beg the reader to accompany me, that he, too, may learn the cause of this expenditure of gunpowder.

The armoury was a large hall, capable of holding with ease several hundred persons. There was a long dining-table in the centre used for committees, courts-martial, &c. &c. At one end of this table stood Q.E.D., at the other Brigadier Littlesole, each being surrounded by his partisans and friends; the rest of the hall was pretty well filled by officers of both services, and a number of railway officials and others, who had all bent their steps thither with the hope of satisfying a common curiosity.

When the place was pretty well full, Mr. Dormouse, holding up a large official-looking document in his hand, said in a loud voice—

'I have requested your attendance here today, gentlemen, for the purpose of reading out in your presence a notification just received from the supreme government, appointing me to succeed to the vacant office of Prefect, so lately filled by our lamented and esteemed friend.'

He then gave the notification to the secretary, Mr. Chutney Tittlebat, and desired him to read it out, which he did in a loud voice.

'No. $\frac{104692}{178650}$.

'*Notification Extraordinary, Fort William, June* 12, 1857.

'The Governor-General in Council is pleased to appoint Quintilian Edward Dormouse, C.S., Special Commissioner of the Central Indian Provinces, with full power to control all civil and military operations, and to conduct in general the administration of the country known as the Central Indian Provinces, until further orders, anything heretofore provided notwithstanding.'

A murmur of approbation ran round the hall from all the friends of the Dormouse party.

Brigadier Littlesole's partisans were calm and self-confident; they turned their eyes upon their chief, and he, looking round with a benignant smile, handed Major Trumps an official document in shape and size very like that still displayed in the hands of Mr. Chutney Tittlebat, and said:—

'Have the goodness, Major Trumps, to read that; and may I beg you, gentlemen,' he added, turning round and waving his hand in a majestic manner, 'to listen.'

'No. $\frac{104692}{178650}$.

'*Notification Extraordinary, Fort William,*
June 12, 1857.

'The Governor-General in Council is pleased to appoint Brigadier John Henry Leviathan Littlesole, C.B., Special Commissioner of the Central Indian Provinces, with full power to control all civil and military operations, and to conduct in general the administration of the country known as the Central Indian Provinces, till further orders, the said provinces being under martial law, anything heretofore provided notwithstanding.'

It was now the turn of the brigadier's party to chuckle, and chuckle they did. Of course the double salute was no longer a mystery, and there being nothing further to do or say, the two special commissioners retired to their respective quarters, along, the one with his secretary, the other with his brigade-major, to issue orders and write letters.

The next morning the following proclamations in the Hindoostanee language appeared posted up in different parts of the city, and circulated throughout the district:—

'Know all men,—That certain designing and evil-disposed men, having seduced the faithful soldiers and servants of the State from their allegiance, and persuaded them to take up arms against the British government:

'Notice is hereby given, that any sepoys returning to their allegiance within six months from the date of this proclamation shall receive a free pardon.

'(Signed) QUINTILIAN EDWARD DORMOUSE,
'Special Commissioner,
'Central Provinces.'

The other proclamation ran as follows:—

'Know all men,—That certain designing and evil-disposed persons, having seduced the faithful servants and soldiers of the British government from their allegiance, and instigated them to commit the most horrible and flagrant crimes, every man found with arms in his possession after the date of this proclamation will be considered a rebel against the British government and summarily hanged, and any man who gives information that leads to the conviction of such offenders shall receive a reward of ten rupees.

'(Signed) J. H. L. LITTLESOLE, Brigadier,
'Special Commissioner,
'Central Provinces.'

Copies of both these proclamations were sent down to Calcutta, and in due time returned with the cordial approbation of the supreme government.

Meantime the special commissioners went to work. Brigadier Littlesole erected a large gallows outside the Aurungabad fort, capable of accommodating nine natives at once. Mr. Dormouse opened an office in the high road, where he posted a native civil officer, with a large book and pens and ink, to receive and enter all applications for pardon. I need hardly add that the brigadier's gallows had more applicants than Mr. Dormouse's receiving office.

One morning when Major Trumps and Brigadier Littlesole were busy looking over the proceedings of a court-martial that had just condemned to death by hanging a cook-boy, on a charge of having attempted to poison a family, consisting of Mrs. Jones and three little Jones's, an orderly who was in attendance came in and announced a 'hofficer.'

'Show him in,' said the brigadier.

He started at the apparition that presented itself at the door. A tall fine-looking young fellow, with a vast profusion of hair about his face, very dirty, his clothes actually hanging to his back and legs in shreds, a native turban of blue cloth round his head, and his skin so sunburnt that he looked in complexion more like a native of the East than an Anglo-Saxon, well armed with sword and revolver, presented himself. It was Graham.

'Well, sir, what do you want?' said the brigadier.

'I want a good deal,' said Graham. 'I believe this is the brigadier's quarters. Have I the honour of addressing the brigadier?'

'You have. Be quick and state what you want done.'

'In the first place I want rest; I've just ridden a hundred and eighty miles from Islamabad, and am half dead. I have brought bad news.'

'Bad news, sir! does anyone ever bring

anything else, I should like to know? Bad news! You didn't suppose I expected you to bring good, did you?'

The brigadier here motioned Graham to a seat, and, summoning a servant, desired him to bring wine and water, cold meat and bread instantly. He then turned to renew the conversation with his visitor.

Meantime Major Trumps (the proceedings, finding, and sentence of the court-martial having been signed by the brigadier) gathered up his papers and took his leave, saying, 'He would be back in a moment; he had a little business to attend to:' and so saying he left.

The little business was, returning the proceedings confirmed, and giving the necessary orders for the execution next morning of the cook-boy, who, however, was destined to make his sudden exit out of this world and entrance into another in company with five others. One was a sweeper, who had been detected concealing a rusty knife in his broom; another an ill-looking native, who could give no account of himself, but was proved to have admitted a dog into the fort that afterwards turned out mad; a third had been convicted of loitering near the magazine, with the lens of a telescope in his possession, with the design, no doubt, of blowing up the place by means of the concentrated solar rays; a fourth, a Mahometan, had been convicted of going about instigating a 'jehad,' or holy war, against the infidels by wearing green shoes; and the fifth, one of the Honourable George Gregory's three-rupee police, who went by the nickname of the *three rupeewallas*, and had been caught in the neighbourhood of the fort the night before.

As soon as Major Trumps had left, the brigadier continued the conversation with Graham.

'So you've come from Islamabad?' he said. 'All the country's up, I suppose?'

'Well, not the country exactly—that seems tolerably quiet. Islamabad has gone, I am sorry to say.'

'And you the only survivor? Dear me, dear me!'

'No, thank God, there are many survivors, but they are in a bad way. I have come to solicit instant aid; a party of Europeans despatched at once may be in time to save the lives of almost all the ladies and children.'

'Impossible to spare a man,' said the brigadier, shaking his head; 'but tell us all about it.'

And so Graham told the whole story from first to last, which I need not repeat here.

In the middle of it Major Trumps returned,

and both the brigadier and he listened with breathless interest.

'I am very sorry,' said the brigadier, as Graham concluded, and turned to help himself to some cold meat and wine and water, which had meantime been brought. 'I am very sorry it is quite impossible for me to help you. No doubt long before this General Codshead will have sent troops from Mitterpore: he is much more favourably situated than I am; he has no fort to protect. Here am I, you see, with a mere handful of men—a mere handful—and this enormous fort to protect.'

'But,' urged Graham, 'the case is most pressing; I was in hopes you would order out a party at once. I am ready to start at once to show them the nearest road there: it is most urgent, I assure you. That little band of helpless innocents, ladies and children, will be sacrificed to a fate that it is impossible even to think of without shuddering, unless instant aid is sent them. Indeed, sir, it is most urgent.'

'It is not for you, sir, to dictate to me what is urgent and what is not urgent,' said the brigadier hastily. 'To diminish by one man the garrison of a beleaguered fort like this would be madness; it is altogether out of the question. After all I do not see that your friends are so much worse off than others. It is merely a question of time; perish we all must. We are surrounded, beset on all sides; as for any of us escaping out of this hobble, it is ridiculous to regard such a result in any way but as most improbable, if not impossible. It is merely a question of time; cut all our throats will be; it's a toss up who goes first, but cut they all will be, that is certain.'

'Give me fifty Europeans mounted on camels, brigadier, and I'll lay a wager no one's throat is cut between this and Islamabad—that is, if I only get there in time.'

'Fifty European soldiers! Mr. Graham, I wouldn't part with a corporal's party from the fort if I was to be hanged the next moment for refusing. Indeed there is no "if" in the case: either hanged or shot we shall all be sooner or later,—not a man leaves this fort while I command it.'

'Good heavens!' said Graham, alternating between a paroxysm of rage, indignation, and despair; 'leave your countrymen to be butchered at Islamabad, brigadier! You cannot be in earnest?'

'Never more so. What! am I likely to be joking? Is it a time for joking, Mr. Graham, while the grave is yawning beneath your feet and the noose is round your neck? Tell me, is that a time for joking? Major Trumps, do you consider that a fit time for joking?'

'Certainly not, sir.'

'And do you consider, Major Trumps, that the grave is *not* yawning beneath your feet? Do you mean to tell me the noose is not round your neck? Do you mean to say we shall not have our throats cut?'

'Not necessarily, sir; but I think it's very likely we shall all be poisoned.'

'Poisoned! of course we shall be poisoned. Have not Mrs. Jones and the three little Jones's been poisoned already, and why should we not be poisoned? I say, what is there to prevent our being poisoned—or hanged? Do you see anything to prevent it, Major Trumps?'

'Certainly not, sir.'

'Of course not, nor does anyone: it is a mere question of time.'

Graham had not been long in taking, mentally, the measure of his two new friends' characters. He very soon saw how the wind lay there, and made up his mind at once how to act; but, being dreadfully worn out and in want of refreshment, he determined to make the best use of his time and opportunities, and now that he had the means of getting a good meal, to make the most of them; and then, having satisfied his craving appetite, to start upon the course of action he had resolved to take. The military gods being so unpropitious he would turn to the civil. So abandoning all hopes of getting any assistance from the narrow-minded selfish coward before him, he asked, with difficulty indeed speaking respectfully—

'Pray who is the chief civil authority here?'

'Civil authority, sir? There is no such thing,' replied the brigadier; 'the country is under martial law, and all the functions of civil government are merged in the military.'

'This is unfortunate,' thought Graham, 'if true.'

'But what has become of all the civilians? there used to be a great many here at the seat of government. Surely they are not all swept away?'

'Swept away?—yes, every vestige of them; that is, officially. Individually, they are all here. Of course you know Mr. Gregory is dead?'

'And his successor?'

'I tell you he has no successor. The civil government is defunct. It is all military government here, and that will be defunct too shortly—it is merely a question of time.'

Keeping to his point—and, what was much more difficult, keeping his temper—Graham at last managed to discover that what remained of the civil administration was vested in the person of Mr. Quintilian Edward Dormouse, and to him he resolved to apply without loss of time. So, saying he would go and look after his camel and attendant, and thanking the brigadier for the hearty meal he had given him, Graham took his leave.

He was not long in finding out the head-quarters of the civil government, and was courteously received by Mr. Q. E. Dormouse, to whom he told his tale very much as he had done to the brigadier, coupling with it the account of the refusal of assistance he had met with, and adding that he hoped Mr. Dormouse would take a wider view of the subject, and see the necessity of despatching a party at once to the relief of his friends.

'Indeed,' said Mr. Dormouse, 'I assure you, Mr. Graham, I fully sympathise with you in your anxiety to hurry to the assistance of your friends. I will do all in my power, and that at once. Unfortunately, you see, I have no control over the European portion of the garrison; otherwise, great as would be the risk of diminishing our garrison during the continuance of the siege, I should at once send a strong party of troops. But, to be frank with you, I have no power whatever in military matters. The brigadier is obstinate—very obstinate; but I'll tell you what I can do. There is a large portion of our civil police lately broken up. It is true they did mutiny in a way, but it was merely the force of circumstances—a little excitement: it is all over now. I have the best information, and am assured that they are all only too eager to return to their duty, and to be taken into the garrison of the fort. I had an application only yesterday, saying that there were exactly a thousand of them here ready to come in, if I would only admit them into the fort. With that strange spirit of clanship which is so strong a characteristic of the native mind, they refuse to come unless they are all admitted at the same time. Well, you may imagine how very distressing it was to me to be thwarted in a measure that would go farther than anything else towards settling the country and restoring confidence—you may imagine, Mr. Graham, I say, how distressing it was to be thwarted: but when I agreed to their conditions, the brigadier, with that arrogance'—Mr. Dormouse here suddenly checked himself—'the brigadier, for reasons best known to himself, absolutely refused to allow them to enter the fort. Of course, all negotiations were broken off, and the men remained in the category of enemies and rebels. But

I am sure that a large body of them—say five hundred—would accompany you and render excellent service. Besides, I have every reason to know that the country is settling down fast. My proclamation, thwarted as it has been in a degree by the ill-judged measures of severity—the crimes, I may say, of irresponsible power, has nevertheless had a very extended effect. The police, I am sure, will do all you require—they are thoroughly trustworthy.'

Poor Graham's heart sank within him as he listened to this proposition, and drew a fancy picture in his imagination of his arrival at the head of five hundred native police to the rescue of his friends! He remained silent. Just as Mr. Dormouse had finished speaking a stranger entered.

'Here's just the man I want to see,' said the special commissioner. 'Come along, let me introduce you: Mr. Bowlemover, Mr. Graham.'

They bowed.

'Mr. Graham has a sad story to tell; Bowlemover, what do you say?' He then gave his friend an outline of Graham's story.

As he was telling it, Graham scanned the features and figure of the new comer with an anxious eye. Somehow or other there was that in his face that gave the young soldier comfort. 'This fellow will help me,' he thought; 'I see it in him.' As Mr. Dormouse finished, Bowlemover jumped up.

'I'll manage it,' he said—'just the thing for me. I'm deuced tired of this infernal fort, Dormouse, and shall be only too glad to get out of it, especially as I shall be able to do some good. I hope we shall not be too late. When can you travel, Mr. Graham?'

'To-night,' said Graham. 'Now, I'm ready now, if I can only get another camel. For God's sake, if you have anything to propose, be quick; you do not know how many lives each minute lost may lose.'

'All right—now I'll tell you. I know there are a whole lot of these railway chaps, and some of Tupper's volunteers, who'll be delighted to go with us. Now, do you stay here and rest a bit; I'll see to it, and make all preparations. We'll muster thirty or forty, or more, and start this evening at sunset.'

Graham stood up to grasp his hand and pour forth his thanks; but his physical powers were utterly prostrated by the tremendous fatigue and exposure he had undergone, and the sudden alternation from despair to hope was too much for his feelings to sustain. He sank down on his chair, pressed his hands to his face, and with difficulty concealed all outward signs of the emotion that thrilled through him.

Bowlemover looked at Dormouse, pointed silently to Graham, and, nodding as if he would have said 'Take care of him,' hurried off whistling to call for volunteers and get his expedition ready.

CHAPTER XLIII.

It is a dangerous thing for a young and beautiful married woman to allow herself to hold clandestine interviews with a stranger of the opposite sex unknown to her husband. Who can tell whither the path may lead that turns off at ever so acute an angle from the road to virtue? Who shall dare to say, so many paces will I walk in it, and then recede? Out of all the crimes that ever were committed since Adam fell, how many were foreseen? Was not Eve herself first contented with the appearance of the forbidden fruit? She did not contemplate tasting it till she had first seen, admired, then wished for it. Leila certainly had no notion when she first countenanced the approach of the stranger what their intimacy would end in.

By degrees she became more accustomed to receiving the visits of the man, whom I shall now call the Mirza. Fired as her soul was by enthusiasm and zeal for what she supposed to be the cause of Islam, entranced by the dazzling idea that she was fated—how high and glorious a destiny!—to take a large share in the re-establishment and supremacy of the faith for which she would at any time willingly have laid down her life—animated by ideas of this sort, she entertained no thought or feeling of a baser kind. All pure herself, she had no suspicion of impurity in others. Inspired by religious hopes and fears, she had no sympathy for emotions of a more earthly nature; and so it came to pass that symptoms which women are always the first to see and to detect in the other sex passed unnoticed. Had it not been for this, the innumerable intimations by gesture, voice, and look that betray the existence of passion would have warned her woman's heart of danger near.

Let not, however, the English reader, accustomed to all the habits and customs of western civilization, be too ready to sit in judgment and utter harsh sentence against Leila. I can better compare her to the bird we read of, that, bewitched by the gaze of the basilisk, falls an easy prey to its deadly enemy, than anything else, and I could more easily describe the means by which the basilisk entranced the bird than the effects of the enchantment upon her. The means were simple, not differing in kind from those we may see exercised every day of our lives if we choose to look—not differing in kind, only in degree. The Mirza understood his art and was well practised. He understood it better than nine hundred and ninety-nine out of a thousand of those who make profession of it, and she was more susceptible than nine hundred and ninety-nine out of a thousand of those who are generally selected, either by real votaries of science or by impostors, as subjects for experiment, or dupes to deceive the public.

I am no believer in the charlatanical nonsense of clairvoyance and electro-biology, yet I most assuredly believe that these grand impostures have been erected on a solid foundation of truth. Nor is it always easy to discern exactly the line where truth ends and imposture begins. It is certain that some minds have power over others, and can acquire it in proportion to the extent to which one chooses to subject itself to the influence of the other. I do not mean to imply that the Mirza mesmerised his victim; he was an adept in mesmerism as in all other kinds of charlatanry, and he had studied the art of mystifying his fellow-creatures in every school almost in the world. All the treasures, whether of real science or imposture, were at his fingers' ends. And so deeply had he studied, and so long and often practised, that he would have found it no easy matter to define where one ended and the other began. So many were his accomplishments, so many were the things he could do, that you would be induced to suppose there was nothing he could not do. He could put a child under a basket on the ground in the presence of spectators, and then stab it through and through, while you heard the cries of the dying child and saw the blood flowing in streams from under the basket, which he would lift up, and lo! there would be nothing there; he could cut a man in two and make him one again; he could swallow knives, eat fire, seize poisonous serpents in his hands and twist them round his neck, or let them coil round and round in his hair till they disappeared ; he could show you himself suspended and seated in mid air, and thousands of other wonderful things, to enumerate which would fill a volume ; but more than this, he could talk of the mysteries of real science in a way that showed he had studied deeply. Especially in the healing art was his knowledge great and practical; the most dangerous diseases he could grapple with; for all he had some device, some mode of treatment ready at hand—not always successful, for then he would have been superhuman; he was only a man, but a very clever one, a most ambitious one, with vast capabilities, untiring energy, immense physical powers, and mental resources, which had never during his lifetime bcen tested to the bottom; and withal he was utterly devoid of all principles save one —self-worship. Add to this that his audience, his patients, his victims, his dupes, his worshippers, were untutored and semi-barbarous, wrapt in sensuality and superstition and prone to credulity, and you might have ceased to wonder at his success had it been even greater than it was.

Yet are these moral giants that we sometimes meet with but weak mortals after all. The Mirza, with all his powers of mind that nature had so lavishly bestowed on him and art had cultivated, was a slave to passion, and that not of the purest or most ennobling kind. Leila thought herself in some way destined to be the bride of heaven, and the man who worshipped her, a being she herself worshipped, something little short of an emanation from the deity himself. Nothing else but this could have blunted her woman's instinct, and blinded her woman's eyes. Else she must have noticed that glance expressing all the intensity of longing desire fixed not seldom on her: the trembling of his whole frame when she touched him ever so lightly, the fondness for remaining in her presence, the reluctance to leave it, the beating heart and quickened breath when in some of the innumerable pursuits they followed out together he bent over her or she bent over him, till the fragrance from her perfumed hair or robes floated like a cloud over his entranced senses. Was it as an ethereal being or destined bride of heaven that he imprinted that burning kiss upon her hand each time he visited and left her? Was it with the simple adoration of a pure heart and a platonic love that he knelt at her feet when he could frame an excuse for doing so, and once kissed the hem of her robe? So free herself from the influence of any such material passion, Leila dreamed not that the wonderful being who now was her too constant companion had aught but the purest feelings towards her. Under his guidance she had travelled over regions where every step they took opened out some fresh wonder to her hitherto untaught mind. She had thirsted eagerly all her life long for knowledge exactly of that sort the stranger had offered in overflowing endless draughts to her lips: she drank and drank, and still the fountain seemed exhaustless, and her desire still unquenchable.

Never but once had the slightest ray of suspicion gleamed upon her woman's heart. Once and once only had it flashed across her mind, and then the idea was indignantly repelled, and that was when the plot was laid for Amy's capture. She had longed for the tree of knowledge, and she found it in him in the fullest and completest sense.

Either deeming that at last the time was come when he could venture to pluck the fruit ripened by his own arts, or, it may be, carried away by the violence of passion, which is proverbially blind, he one evening ventured to hint to Leila his aspirations after happiness of rather more material nature than he had in his lessons held out to her as the end and aim of all existence. She started and blushed, but the hint was very slight, and the emotion caused by it proportionately so.

Misinterpreting the cause of the blush that crimsoned her cheeks, or carried away by feeling, he went on, and said—

'That union, fairest Leila, between two loving hearts, such as ours, is ever blessed by heaven: nay, it is but the fulfillment of destiny. When mortals are created by Alla, they are created in pairs, sent into the world each to follow out its own destiny, till the happy period arrives when they cross one another's path; then they recognise their common origin. Like two streams mingling their waters together in one channel, they become united; like two rays of light blending into one, their unity is complete. The temporary separation caused by the accident or circumstances of life acting on their material bodies, fades away. The soul asserts its power, and yields to the inevitable commands of nature. She will not be disobeyed. As well might the air I move my hand through, thus, refuse to let it pass as the soul refuse to acknowledge the unity of its existence with its fellow when providence has brought them into contact. We two were thus created, destined to be one. When first I saw you, I recognised the being that providence had called into existence simultaneously with myself—to be part of myself. Against this mysterious ordinance of nature human laws and customs are powerless. Yield, then, Leila, loveliest of women, whom my soul worships with the fondest, deepest devotion—yield to destiny! Fly with me from this land, from this life you lead—a life that stagnates all the powers and feelings of the soul—to your own native hills, where, hand in hand, untrammelled by the arbitrary laws of tyrants made to fetter in hard bondage the minds that nature destined to be free, we will wander among the haunts of your childhood. There, dwelling always together, I will live with you and for you only; I will unfold still further than I have done the book of knowledge; I will teach you the mysteries of the heavenly bodies, and show you new worlds, where beings you have never dreamed of revel in the enjoyment of immortal life. I will teach you to become still more acquainted with the mysteries of this world's creation and its treasures. I will open out to your mind new realms of science of whose depth, and extent, and beauty, and magnificence, you can have no idea. I will teach and elevate your mind till, growing daily more pure and more ethereal, you at length become fitted for that perfect union which cannot be attained by ordinary mortals, but which the favourite children of nature are created for, and shall attain, if only they refuse not to embrace their destiny.'

He ceased speaking for a moment. She raised her eyes, till then cast down, to his, and gazed full into his face, as if with those large liquid orbs she would penetrate into his inmost heart. The passionate lover cannot exercise the power of the will over the being before whom he prostrates himself in humble adoration. For the moment the spell was broken, and Leila held the vantage ground. She said—

'You are teaching me a new lesson this evening, Mirza—different, oh how different!—from those I loved to listen to before. Speak no more in this strain, for something in my breast warns me to close my ears. To you indeed I owe everything; you have taught me that which has given life a value it never had before. Is there poison lurking too in this cup that I have drunk from so freely from your hand? Where is the destiny you spoke of if I return to my native, my beloved country? Where is the destiny to be fulfilled in this? You have told me, that by my hand Alla would work out the destruction of the infidel and the restoration of Islam to its old glories. For this I am willing—willing! Oh how thankful should I be to sacrifice all life has to offer! and for such an end a sacrifice must be made: but for that you propose—indeed, I understand it not. Are there no obligations binding on a wife?'

'You are right, Leila,' he said; 'you have corrected me, you have checked my too hasty aspirations. I was looking forward, dazzled by the brilliant future I beheld in my mind's eye, forgetting that you cannot see what is made plain to me, revealed by Divine inspiration.' Then he added, after a pause—

'The scheme I have foretold will be worked out by destiny, and yours will be the share you hope for; but I looked beyond the present. I was too impatient; for the moment too much under the influence of mere human mortal weaknesses—too eager to reap the reward, to pluck the fruit that will, if left alone, ripen and fall into my lap. The same power that directs and controls the course of the heavenly bodies in their everlasting march, controls human events and human destinies, and will lead two loving hearts in its own time to blend together into one. Leila,' he added, clasping and pressing to his lips her hand which, overpowered by surprise and the suddenness of his movement, she allowed to linger in his, and the next instant passing his strong arm round her slender waist, 'Leila, you are mine—mine only—my pupil—nay, my goddess, my love. Destiny, stern to other mortals, is kind—ah, how kind!—to us; for it has united us. Let us only forestall the time by a few short months. Fly—fly with me this night. With me you shall be what Alla intended you to be—a queen.'

She struggled to free herself; he held her, grasped as in a vice—she was powerless as a child. She tried to speak, but emotion prevented her; or was it the power of that desperate iron-like will pouring its force through those firelit eyes of his, that, fixed full on her, seemed to demand the obedience of a slave? At first as the blood rushed up to her face she blushed crimson—her shoulders, her neck, her forehead, were all flushed—her heart beat wildly—he could feel its feverish throbs as he pressed her to his bosom, and each throb sent a thrill of livelier passion through him: then she grew pale, pale as the white rose in her hair, pale as her own snowy robe, save for the red spot of anger in her cheek; still she could not speak: she was spell-bound, condemned to pay the penalty of her imprudence, and listen all helplessly still longer to that voice pouring its moral poison into her ears.

'A queen, Leila! The fairest queen on all the earth, and the most powerful, for your slave shall be one who never yet found his equal and never will find him and suffer him to live a rival on the earth. And know this,' he added, passing from entreaty to threat, 'refuse my offer or yield to my prayers, it is all one—you are mine, and never shall escape my hands. Drive me from your presence with scorn, and I return to it a conqueror in triumph. He you call your husband has but a few days to live. At one word, at one sign from me, the whole district rises in revolt. That word will be spoken, that sign given, when the hour comes; the next time I visit you I shall come as a conqueror, and you will be free to reward me with your love, untrammelled by those bonds of human law which you fancy separate us now and make you another's for ever. Say you will not force me to violence—say you will be mine—say you yield—you must, for I WILL it—now——'

The gradual cessation of her powers of physical resistance he had attributed to the growing obedience of her will: the subsidence of effort, the symptom only of fainting strength on her part, he interpreted into acquiescence. He was deceived; the recoil was in proportion to the prostration. Her powers of endurance had ebbed like the sea at spring-tide; like the sea at spring-tide was its flood—on and on, overpowering all obstacles, confident in its own overwhelming motive force, the impulse communicated by the powers of nature—on it came with a bound, and with a bound such as he was totally unprepared for—a force he had no idea that slender yet exquisitely proportioned frame could exercise. She tore herself from his grasp, regained her feet, and stood at a few paces from him, glaring, panting like a tigress that has seized its prey in the act of despoiling her of her young. With her hands clenched, her lips firmly compressed together and white as alabaster, her bosom heaving with emotion regularly yet rapidly, she stood the image and ideal of outraged virtue glaring upon vice. Then those thin white lips opened —to address him, to speak words of endearance, of entreaty, of love? No—she uttered a cry—a cry of agony—a wail of distress like that shipwrecked sailors are said sometimes to hear amid the roaring sea that surges over them before they are engulphed in its black hissing waters—a wail from the spirit of the storm. It was heard by her attendants; it was heard through the length and breadth of that large rambling place; it penetrated the most distant apartments and reached the ears of her husband as he sat in his own chamber busy with his counsellors. Then might be heard voices outside, and steps hurrying along the corridor: and among the first that reached her chamber was the Nawab. With him entered, close following on his heels, the chief of the eunuchs, Sidi Gulzar; then women and attendants, servants, soldiers, guards. There was a strange look about the eunuch's face, and a twinkle in his eyes, but no one noticed him: they had eyes only for their beautiful mistress. There she lay the image of death upon her silken couch; besides her there was no one else present.

'Water, water!' shouted the Nawab as he raised her gently in his arms, seeing at once that she had fainted.

They brought him water cooled with ice in a silver goblet; he dashed it over her face, and shouted 'more—more yet.' Slowly she revives and opens her eyes; at first she stares wildly—vacantly: then, as consciousness returns, raises her head slightly from the recumbent position it occupied on his arm, and gazes timidly round the room, scans the furthermost corner, looks into every anxious face about her—for by this time her attendants are crowding round—and finally rests her eyes on her husband.

She gazed at him for a moment, and then, throwing her arms round his neck and burying her face in his bosom, she burst into a passionate flood of tears.

It was long before she could recover the least control over herself. Thinking a cooling draught might relieve her, the Nawab ordered Sidi Gulzar to go and fetch a cup of sherbet, at the same time that he directed all the attendants present to leave. By-and-by Sidi Gulzar brought the sherbet, placed it beside his master, and with a low obeisance left them.

The Nawab took up the goblet and held it to her lips. She had ceased weeping, and was becoming more calm; but no sooner had her lips touched the liquid in the cup than she started back, and raising her eyes, wild with excitement, to her husband, she cried out in an hysteric scream, 'And you too!' and burst out weeping afresh.

The Nawab was puzzled. Never before in his whole life had he seen her in such a state. The only time that she seemed the least calmed was when he bent over her, pressed his lips against her forehead, and whispered into her ears soft words of love and tenderness, such as a fond husband may whisper to his wife.

CHAPTER XLIV.

When the Nawab sent his men out to the Kooria hills, on the pretence of protecting his district from the incursions of dacoits or banditti—in reality to get them out of the way while the English officers and their families removed from his palace to a place of greater safety—he little thought the feigned danger was so soon to become a real one.

The profession of banditti called dacoitee is one of the regular and time-honoured institutions of India. As in England in old times, and in Ireland and Scotland more recently—in fact, in every country in the world but little advanced in civilisation—no stigma whatever attached to the profession of the hereditary robber. His father and his forefathers, from time immemorial, had been robbers before him; as a matter of course, he followed in their steps. But while this system was common to other countries besides India, it was perhaps a peculiar feature of Indian dacoitee that it was ostensibly and systematically supported by the different independent states. A band of dacoits may have been located in a certain territory, they and their forefathers, for a century—perhaps for centuries. They possessed strongholds, forts, castles, or impregnable positions among the mountains, from which it was difficult, nay impossible, to dislodge them. The ruler of the territory in whose domains they were settled never molested them. They paid him a certain tribute and enjoyed immunity. On the other hand, they never molested their protecting sovereign, under whose shelter, negatively at any rate, they dwelt. They carried their raids into neighbouring territories; but within the boundaries of that they called their own, life and property were secure.

This state of things has lasted in India for many hundred years. The Mahometan sovereigns, in the palmy day of the empire, to a certain extent checked the evil, and suppressed the system of dacoitee, but it survived all their endeavours to eradicate it, and it was only when the Mahometan empire was succeeded by the British government that any effectual progress was made in putting it down. The efforts of our government have been to a considerable extent successful; still the system is suppressed rather than rooted up. It is ready to break out again in full vigour the moment the iron grasp that holds it down is relaxed or removed. It is not to be wondered at, therefore, that when the mutiny took place and the government for the time was pretty well broken up all over the country, dacoitee sprang to life again in a moment, as if reinvigorated by a magic impulse. And the effects of the rebellion were traceable in the revival of this institution long after they had disappeared from every other part or system of the country or the government.

There was a noted dacoit or leader of banditti named Doonghur Rao, who had lived as his forefathers had lived, and found protection under the predecessor of the Nawab of Islamabad. There, as elsewhere, the iron grasp of the British government had suppressed the gang, and Doonghur Rao had now for many years been living, as far as was generally known or believed, a peaceful and quiet life on his own estate among the Kooria hills. How he employed himself and spent his time, to what pursuits he devoted the energies of his restless disposition, no one exactly knew. Mr. Dacres had long had his eye on him, but could never detect any sign of guilty complicity in any robberies committed in the neighbouring districts, or in his own division. Indeed, so high an opinion had he of the old robber chief that, since the outbreak had occurred, he had many and many a time thought of throwing himself upon him for protection. It was a course not to be resorted to till the last; but if everything else failed, he was resolved, if possible, to carry out this scheme. Once in Doonghur Rao's fort and hands, however, the whole party would have been as much at his tender mercies as the sheep in the shambles is in the power of the butcher. It was a dangerous expedient; it might be successful, or it might be eminently disastrous. It was not to be thought of, except as a last resource.

Doonghur Rao, however, was not long in declaring himself. The conspirators who had set this gigantic mutiny on foot counted well each resource that would be open to them, and no doubt they knew that the dacoitee system would be one. It was their object to involve the whole country as much as possible in confusion, to throw down as many of the landmarks of order and government as possible, and then out of the chaos to reconstruct an empire supported on the bayonets of the soldiers. The sudden revival of dacoitee, therefore, in every corner of the land, was no unimportant feature in the scheme.

It was, as I have said, one of the essentials

of the system in its perfect state that a good understanding should exist between the leader of banditti and the chief or sovereign of the territory in which he lived; it was a compact mutually acknowledged to be binding on both sides; and we may be sure, if broken by one, certain to be broken by the other. As long as Doonghur Rao was unmolested by the Nawab of Islamabad he was not likely to molest the life and property of the Nawab's retainers or subjects. Should the Nawab, however, proceed against the dacoit, the latter would not hesitate to make reprisal. Under the old *régime* the Nawab would not have dared to attempt so dangerous a task as that of suppressing Doonghur Rao's power single-handed. And it is probable that, could he have foreseen what was to occur, Kooria was the last direction in which he would have sent his troops. But at that time he had heard nothing of the old dacoit leader's intention of returning to his old profession; and the latter, though surprised at first that the Nawab should attempt what in former days neither he nor his predecessors would have ventured on, easily accounted for it in his own mind by the reports which prevailed everywhere that the Nawab was the staunch ally of the British government.

He would have found out indeed, had he

waited and enquired, that, however disposed the Nawab might be to cast in his lot with the paramount power, his men were actuated by vastly different motives. But there was no time for enquiry. Doonghur Rao had everything ready for raising his standard, so to call it, long before the mutiny of the troops at Islamabad lit up the flame of rebellion in that part of the country. This event was the signal for him to act. The gang were all collected ready at hand; the first moment they flew to arms, at the call of their old hereditary chieftain, they found to their astonishment, and certainly to his, that their old protector, their hereditary sovereign and feudal lord, the Nawab, had occupied the passes with an armed force, apparently with every intention of acting against them.

Doonghur Rao's men, who had for years been chafing under the restraint imposed on them, were only too eager to indulge their old habits, and 'their swords in their scabbards,' as they expressed it in Oriental metaphor, 'actually thirsted to taste blood.' It is no matter of surprise then that, finding a body of armed men professedly sent against them, and to all appearance really ready to act in a hostile manner, they paused not to ask questions, but attacked at once. Blood was shed, happily for our friends the refugees, for that bloodshed was the means of averting from them an immediate assault, which in their then condition would undoubtedly have ended fatally. Nothing but this could have kept the Nawab's men from returning from Kooria the morning after they got there, when they found that their victims had escaped, and completing their destruction. The feeling too that they had been duped, and made the victims of a trick by their own chief, made them especially anxious to wipe out the insult in the blood of the defenceless and innocent Feringhees. But no sooner had it become apparent that they had been duped, and that the party of English officers had not been, and had entertained no intention of going, to the place in which the ambuscade was set, and before they had had time to give vent to their anger even in words, they were called to attention by the voice of their chief, and found themselves assailed on all sides by a vigorous assault of Doonghur Rao's men. The old warrior knew well the advantage of being the first to act on the offensive. His information was of the best, his men only too willing; and about the grey of the morning, when men and horses are apt to be particularly drowsy, and when it is difficult to distinguish objects at a distance, with a shout and a yell such as they had often uttered before on similar occasions, the dacoit's men rushed, sword in hand, upon the camp of the Nawab's troops.

Blood having been once shed—and there was a good deal spilt on that occasion—the Nawab's retainers felt it a point of honour to have their revenge before they proceeded against the enemy they were all longing to confront, viz. the English refugees. And to this accident, if I may call it so, Dacres and his party owed their immunity from attack and annoyance for many days after they had taken up their abode in the Sudder Ameen's house.

It is worth while just to glance at the state of affairs and parties in the small territory of Islamabad at this crisis, for it affords an excellent illustration of the chaotic and disordered condition in which all that part of India which was affected by the revolt was thrown. There was the Nawab in the first place, well disposed himself towards the British government, but timid and uncertain how to act, and fearful of the consequence of his actions on whichever side he went. There was even in his own house a powerful faction arrayed against him, though as yet in secret. There were the English refugees—a small party all together in one house, stronger than they looked, on account of their spirit, their unity of feeling, their skill, and their prestige. There was a large part of the Nawab's own retainers, ready enough to act against their own lord and master if they could gain their object, the destruction of the English, in no other way than by first destroying him; and, finally, there was the daring dacoitee band, under Doonghur Rao, of whom it may safely be asserted that their hands were against every man, and every man's hand against them.

It is obvious that if any two of this faction coalesced, they would have an overwhelming advantage against any of the rest. If Dacres could have communicated with Doonghur Rao, and got him over to his side, the party of officers and ladies would, as I have said before, have been quite safe from everyone but Doonghur Rao. But Dacres hesitated to commit himself. There was, however, another character who played no unimportant part upon the scene, who saw the advantages he could gain, and determined to play for them. It was the Mirza.

The sudden attack just described had been followed by a reprisal, and the desultory kind of warfare native troops when left to their own devices are so fond of. Doonghur Rao could do but little till he had removed the great impediment to freedom of action—the regular troops of the Nawab, now posted in an impregnable situation. It was not easy to overpower them, for they had taken up a position in the hills from which it was difficult to dislodge any large body of men who had ever so little wish to fight. Doonghur Rao had occupied an equally strong post himself, and was equally safe; but action, not inaction, was his object, while the rebels cared not how long they waited for the revenge they were determined to have, so that it came at last. To Doonghur Rao this obstacle was to the last degree irritating. He was afraid to turn his back on his foe, and set out to plunder the country behind him, lest he should be followed up, his own cattle and estates destroyed, and himself attacked at a disadvantage. On the other hand, he was not as yet strong enough to force a passage through the enemy's lines. Many days passed while matters were in this condition, and in this condition they were when the Mirza, the morning after the interview related above, rode into the dacoit's camp.

No need to delay this narrative to relate the interview between two such kindred spirits as the Mirza and Doonghur Rao. The former felt as confident of fulfilling his design before he entered on it, as he was certain that he bestrode the camel that carried him to the Kooria hills. Such men as Doonghur Rao and Colonel Hussain Khan, the Nawab's commandant, the Mirza knew he could twist round his little finger. Before two hours had elapsed a messenger left Doonghur Rao's camp with a white flag for Colonel Hussain Khan; and half an hour after the latter's chief was closeted in Doonghur Rao's tent, the Mirza making a third, all discussing their common plans, as if they had all been bosom friends for the last twenty years. I need only mention the result. Next morning the two camps were struck, and the two lately hostile forces, each under its own leader, with the Mirza for a counsellor to both, marched, to the stirring sound of harsh drums and still harsher trumpets, towards Islamabad, with the avowed object of compelling the Nawab to place himself ostensibly at their head, to declare war against the British government, and to follow up the declaration by a combined attack upon the English refugees, and the small band of native soldiers that still remained faithful to their colours.

CHAPTER XLV.

MEANWHILE time had sped, as it was likely to with the English refugees under such circumstances. They had not been slow to take advantage of the breathing space afforded them, and had laboured with unremitting exertions to strengthen their position; not unsuccessfully either, for by taking advantage of every facility for defence afforded by locality, by outhouses, garden walls, &c., which Stevens' practised eye at once detected, they had succeeded in making the place so strong a fortification that nothing short of starvation or heavy artillery could drive them out of it. Against the former they had provided by laying in a store of provisions, in which the Nawab helped them most materially, for as yet none of his people, whatever they felt, dared openly to disobey a direct command. Against the latter they could but trust in providence; and if artillery was brought against them and the house was destroyed, they would still hold out for many days in the Saiyad's tomb.

The only drawback to the latter place was the painful suspicion that the knowledge of the subterraneous connection between the tomb and the house was known to those who were likely to take part in the attack. So important was it deemed to clear up all doubts on this head, that Dacres made an express appointment with the Nawab, with whom he still held daily communication, for the purpose of finding out if he knew anything about it. Asgar Ally, when questioned, declared most positively that no one knew of the existence of the underground passage except the owner of the house, who was at Delhi, one of his wives who was also at Delhi, or at least supposed to be there, and himself. It had always, he said, been kept a profound secret by Ali Moorad, and the only way Asgar Ally became acquainted with it was by the treachery of his favourite wife, with whom he had a liaison, and who had been trusted by her lord and master with the secret he as little suspected she would ever betray as her own honour.

There was a good deal of difference of opinion among the officers of the little garrison about this. Murray by no means shared Dacres' confidence in the Nawab's loyalty, and continually urged him not to put his faith in princes; especially not to betray this secret of the passage to the tomb by asking him about it. Thurston too was most eager on Murray's side, but he was especially energetic in his attempt to shake Dacres' confidence in Asgar Ally, a man who had come to be looked upon now as the most useful member of their force; indeed no one but Thurston ever spoke of him but in terms of the most enthusiastic attachment. The ladies grew fond of him, from witnessing constantly his unwearied exertions in their behalf; the children used to call him their dear Asgar Ally, and were delighted beyond all measure when he could spare a minute or two from his multifarious duties to take them one by one upon his back, or go down on his knees and constitute himself an elephant, when at least four of them would scramble up on his back and neck, and be carried about the hall in triumph. I say 'multifarious duties,' for they were multifarious. He was Dacres' right hand man. He it was who ventured out every night and came in before morning with intelligence—intelligence, too, rare virtue!—that Dacres never found to fail. He it was who guided the different foraging parties to spots where provisions were procurable. He did little menial offices whenever he could for any of the officers, or their wives, or the children, all of whom felt the want of servants sadly; he would help to cook the dinner, carry it to table, wait while the meal was being served, get water, bring the gentlemen lights for their pipes, and the next moment go out on an errand of life and death as zealously and readily as if he too had had a white skin, a fair-faced English wife, and two or three little prattling babies. It may readily be understood that Asgar Ally being such a universal favourite, anyone who spoke against him was proportionately unpopular. Thurston, therefore, was forced to keep his opinions pretty much to himself, and advance them, whenever he did advance them, in counsel with Murray and the other officers. That Dacres already suspected Thurston my readers know. He too was alone in his suspicions; no one else shared them, or looked at them in any other light than as most groundless and unjust, had they not been ridiculous. Barncliffe, as a general rule, suspected everybody, and it is no wonder therefore that Asgar Ally came in for a share of his bad opinion; but he was too cautious a man ever to commit himself by saying anything about anybody. He had gone through a great deal of distress and anxiety of a domestic nature ever since the outbreak, his wife having suffered very much in health from the shock occasioned by it, expecting as she was before long to add to the race of Barncliffes.

Believing most implicitly that their deliverance was only a matter of time, and that the only doubt was whether they could hold out till aid arrived either from Mitterpore or from Aurungabad, Dacres' spirits rose daily as he saw their position growing in strength under the efforts that were being made to fortify it. And as so much depended on the fact of the subterranean passage being a secret, known only to a very few, he returned from his clandestine interview with the Nawab, with a load of anxiety off his mind. Without divulging the secret of the communication, he had satisfactorily established the fact that the Nawab had not the slightest suspicion of its existence. They might therefore entertain considerable hope that it was not known, and if forced out of the defences in the house, they might all take refuge there, and elude, at any rate for a time, the vigilance of their pursuers; and even after their retreat had been discovered, as discovered of course it must be in time, their position would be as strong if not stronger than the one they would have just abandoned: the enemy would have all their work to do over again and to commence afresh. 'It is only a question of time,' Dacres said to himself fifty times a day. Over and over again he counted on his fingers the number of days he calculated it would take his messenger to reach Mitterpore, and a party of European soldiers, mounted on the strongest and fleetest camels that were to be had, to reach them. As each day passed away and each night, with no fresh alarm and no fresh disaster, his spirits rose, and he looked more and more confidently to their eventual deliverance from dangers, of which at one time there was scarcely any hope.

They had not been in their new position many days before he found a fresh source of anxiety in the illness of his friend Stevens. His constitution, never very strong, was unable to bear the shock which the late crisis they had passed through and were now experiencing dealt to it. He was a man of deep feeling, and, though no consideration of personal danger would have affected him the least, anxiety on account of his family pressed heavily upon his mind. He had been unwearying in his exertions ever since affairs had assumed their present attitude, and exposed himself to the intense heat of the sun too freely. This, combined with constant labour and ceaseless anxiety, brought on a dangerous illness, and, before the measures for the full defence of their present position, which he had planned, had been completed, the originator of them was prostrated.

The party had many advantages in the Sudder Ameen's house, which they had not in the Nawab's palace; not the least valuable of them was the number of different apartments, which enabled them to live with much greater comfort than when they were all together. The ladies had four rooms between them, and the gentlemen a similar number on the ground floor. When Stevens fell ill, arrangements were gladly made for him to occupy one room with his family, so that he could be kept more quiet, and have the advantage of his wife and sister's uninterrupted attendance. But the sorrows of his afflicted family were far from culminating in Stevens' dangerous illness. He had not been laid up two full days before Mrs. Stevens' deepest anxieties were aroused for her youngest child, who was taken dangerously ill with fever. The disease would not be checked, and within forty-eight hours of its first seizure the mother was weeping over the lifeless body of her little darling. The tears were soon dried, however, for in the condition they were in, and with the prospects they had before them, the peaceful and painless death of the infant could not be viewed in any other light or felt to be anything but a great mercy.

A good many members of the other families about this time fell sick—no doubt in consequence of the exposure and hardships they had gone through, acting upon physical powers but little accustomed to endure them: and now that there was a temporary lull in the storm, that, while it raged around them in all its fury had, by its very violence, kept up the excitement, they began to feel the effects of a reaction.

This is too common a phenomenon to deserve much notice, and we need look no farther for the cause of the great depression and sickness that began to affect so many of the garrison. Mrs. Stevens after the death of her youngest child seemed broken-hearted; her courage and spirits, till now undaunted, entirely gave way; daily, nay hourly, she struggled with the feeling, and, animated by the desire of tending her sick husband to the last, kept at her post till exhausted nature absolutely succumbed, and on Amy devolved the duties of taking care of Georgy and nursing her brother and sister. The old ayah was an invaluable aid, and all their companions were ready with sympathy and assistance. Still matters grew from bad to worse.

Dr. Mactartan had been in to pay his usual evening visit, and Dacres impatiently waited his return. He came out of the room at last, followed by Amy, who was crying, and with difficulty preventing her sobs from being heard.

'How are your patients this evening?' asked Dacres of the medicine man.

He shook his head. 'Both very bad; I scarcely think poor Mrs. Stevens can survive the night. She may be kept up by stimulants, but I do not think there is the least prospect of her ultimate recovery. Oh, for a breath of air a little less stifling than this terrible atmosphere of ninety-eight degrees! Poor lady! And Stevens, too, is no better. Fancy high fever, and the thermometer at ninety-eight day and night—night and day. Who can stand it?'

'You must take care of yourself, Miss Leslie—indeed you must,' said Dacres. 'You are actually worn out with your exertion. Do leave your brother and sister, and go and lie down for a little; to my certain knowledge you have taken no rest for the last four or five days. Now, do; Mrs. Murray will take your place just for an hour or two.'

'Yes, indeed I will,' said that lady, who had come up as Dacres spoke. 'Go, Amy, and lie down, like a good girl. I will call you directly there is the least change.'

Amy felt indeed the need she had of following her friend's advice; but she felt, too, how vain it was to attempt to follow it. Rest! A cool room, quiet and dark, a soft bed or a sofa, might indeed have tempted her to try. But, alas! these things were unknown to most ladies in the disturbed parts of India in 1857. A common counterpane and blanket spread on the stone floor, in a room occupied by three ladies and several children, full of flies, and with the atmosphere so close and hot that it seemed almost impossible to breathe—these were all the appliances there were to tempt poor Amy to rest her aching limbs and throbbing head. No: she would rather sit at the bedside of her two patients and watch their feverish sleep or listen to their faint moanings than try to court sleep upon her wretched pallet. Though she was unwilling however to do this, she sadly wanted a few minutes' conversation with Dacres, for she had easily divined from several unmistakeable signs, such as her companions whispering together, while every now and then furtive glances were directed towards her, that intelligence of some sort, and in some way affecting her, had been received by some one. She said therefore, in reply to Dacres' tender solicitude, that, though it was out of the question her lying down or attempting to sleep, she would be most delighted to take a turn in the garden (for the sun was now gone down) and get a little fresh air. Dacres readily offered to accompany her, only too glad to have an opportunity of doing or saying anything to cheer, in however slight a degree, the gentle girl who had, since their misfortunes set in, won the hearts of all. Alas! he had little to cheer her. The instant the suspicion had entered her mind that her friends had intelligence of some kind they were unwilling to impart to her, it forced itself into a settled conviction that something had happened to Graham. She had been thinking the matter over all the day, as well as she could when her mind was not occupied with other subjects, and the more she thought the more she became convinced that if her friends had anything to conceal from her it could be nothing but what had some reference to Graham. Anxiety at last became overpowering, and she determined to seize the first opportunity of enquiring. So she put a leading question to Dacres as soon as they were alone in the garden.

'Tell me, Mr. Dacres, have you heard anything from Mr. Harley since they started?'

'Nothing,' said Dacres, 'from him, but we have heard something of him—and the news, I am sorry to say, is not good.'

'Were they safe—was Mr. Graham safe? —do tell me.'

'Why, my dear Miss Leslie, you have had so many sorrows to bear that I fear you can, indeed, scarcely bear more. You must be inured to suffering—and yet, sooner or later, you will know the worst.'

'The worst—oh yes! let me know the worst—indeed I can bear it. What have we not gone through the last month—and there is more in store—yes, more in store. Oh God! how long? how much more have we to suffer? Then poor Mr. Graham is lost—I see it in your face. Tell me, what have you heard? This suspense is intolerable. Anything is better—do tell me!'

'Indeed, I think it is better to tell you all. It is on native authority only, remember—it may be false—lest I do but buoy you up with hopes that may only deceive. All I know is this: Asgar Ally brought word this morning, after one of his usual nightly expeditions in search of information, that the dead body of an officer had been seen in the jungle several miles from here, on the Aurungabad road, who had evidently died a natural death—that is, he had not been murdered: and from all we can gather about it we believe—it is most likely—to be poor Graham—that is all.'

'All!'

How much may be expressed in a word! The simple way in which she repeated the little word 'all,' the utter blank despair conveyed in her tone of voice, touched Dacres to the heart. He said nothing, but sent towards heaven a silent prayer that the Father of Mercies would deal tenderly with this wounded heart.

'I will go in now,' she said; 'I do not feel as if I could stand about any longer. Thank you, Mr. Dacres; you have relieved me of one burden at any rate—the burden of suspense.'

Dacres pressed her hand as she turned to go into the house. With difficulty she managed to ascend the steep stone steps that are always found in native houses where there are any steps at all, and resumed her place by the bedside of the patients, permitting Mrs. Murray to go and look after her own little one. That night her labour of watching found diminution, for her sister died. Poor Amy fell upon her neck and sobbed as if her heart would break, but the free flowing of her tears gave her such relief as she had not known for many a day. Stevens was much worse, and little Georgy could only by the greatest difficulty and constant watching be kept from running in to see his papa and mama.

CHAPTER XLVI.

THE following morning Asgar Ally came back with more exciting information than usual. This was nothing less than a rumour that the Nawab's troops had mutinied, plundered the city and palace, and were in full march against them. Like many other reports at that time, it was prophetically rather than actually true. It was the most likely thing to happen, and it was exactly what all men wished, except the few who were well-disposed towards the British government, and it was what everyone saw would happen if reinforcements were not sent soon in the shape of some European troops.

Dacres was talking to Murray and Thurston about this when he heard his name called by some one. It was Barncliffe.

'Hallo, Dacres!' he said, 'here's the kossid (or messenger) come back from Mitterpore.'

'Thank God!' said Dacres, as he hurried to the door, expecting to see the kossid, and behind him a couple of hundred or so of English soldiers, armed with Endfields and mounted on camels. No such thing: the man was alone, and looked as if he had undergone a great deal of suffering, for he was care-worn and haggard to the last degree.

'Ha, my fine fellow!' said Dacres, patting the man on the shoulder, 'you have done right well. What news?—when are the troops to be here?'

'Troops!' said the man—'I saw none.'

'None!' shrieked Dacres. 'None coming? Good God, man! what do you mean?'

'Letter, sahib! I have got a letter,' replied the other.

'Letters be——. Well, let's have them; I suppose they have written to say the detachment was to start next day. Delay for want of carriage, very likely.'

It was a work of time producing these letters, for the sewing of the man's shoes had to be unfastened before they could be produced; but produced they were at last—two large service envelopes, all sealed and franked, and addressed, 'On the Public Service only.'

There were a good many natives standing about, a number of the sepoys and irregulars having been attracted to the spot by the important event of the arrival of the kossid, who was expected by most of them to return with at least a regiment of Europeans and a troop of horse artillery behind him, as well as a battery of siege guns drawn by elephants. Dacres had a kind of presentiment as the man handed him the letters that they would contain intelligence that it would be better to read without native witnesses, at all events. He therefore beckoned those of the officers who had come up, and who wanted to hear the news, to accompany him into one of the rooms. There he opened the letters and read them out. They were as follows, word for word:—

'*From* CAPTAIN BLACKHOLT, *Assistant Adjutant-*
'*General, Mitterpore, to* —DACRES, Esq. C.S.
'*Commissioner, Islamabad.*

'MITTERPORE: *June* —, 1857.

'1. SIR,—I am desired by Major-General Codshead, commanding the Mitterpore division, to inform you that your scrap of a letter, dated Islamabad, ——, forwarded by the kossid, by whom this answer will be sent, has been duly received.

'2. Major-General Codshead begs me to remark that your style of addressing him is exceedingly irregular, and not at all in accordance with the established usages of the service.

'3. With reference to your application for

a detachment of European soldiers to be sent to Islamabad, the Major-General is unable to comply with the request, or to sanction the move of a body of troops to so great a distance without authority from the Commander-in-Chief.

'4. As the sanction of the Supreme Government would be required before His Excellency the Commander-in-Chief could order the march of the detachment, you are requested to forward the following documents, together with an official application for the troops—that is to say, provided the causes which first led you to require their aid be still in existence.

'5. The necessary documents are as follows:—

'A. A statement of the strength of the detachment required.

'B. A statement, supported by committee reports in triplicate, of the barrack accommodation available at Islamabad.

'6. Upon the receipt of these papers, the Major-General will forward the application through the usual channel for the consideration of His Excellency the Commander-in-Chief, and final transmission to Government.

'7. As regards the payment of money promised to the bearer, the Major-General desires me to state that he cannot authorise the disbursement of public money on this account until he has been furnished with an audited bill. You will have the goodness, therefore, to transmit a bill in triplicate for the amount required, which will be sent through this office to Calcutta for audit.

'I have the honour to be, Sir,
'Your most obedient servant,
'GEORGE BLACKHOLT, *Captain*,
'*Assistant Adjutant-General*,
'*Mitterpore Division.*

'P.S.—I beg to enclose a reply from Captain Constantine Grambag, relative to the carriage and conveyances alluded to in your note.'

The other letter was as follows:—

'*From* CAPTAIN GRAMBAG, *Assistant Commissary-General, to* CAPTAIN BLACKHOLT, *Assistant Adjutant-General.*

'MITTERPORE: *June* —, 1857.

'SIR,—I have the honour to acknowledge the receipt of your letter No. 5,867 A, Book Z, and enclosures; and in reply to state, for the information of Mr. Dacres, Commissioner of Islamabad, that it will be necessary for him to forward to this office indents in duplicate, countersigned by the officer commanding this station, before I can furnish him with the conveyances required for the use of the women and children alluded to in the enclosure of your letter. It will also be necessary to forward hire in advance for the cattle, whatever species of carriage may be required, in accordance with Sec. XCIV. Par. XV. Chap. XVIII. of the Standing Regulations.

'I have the honour to be, Sir,
'Your most obedient servant,
'CONSTANTINE GRAMBAG, *Captain*,
'*Assistant Commissary-General.*'

Language would fail to describe the indignation, the disgust, the despair, that seized the few listeners to the above letters. As for Dacres, he actually cried with emotion, partly rage, partly scorn, partly indignation, to think that he and all about him—those tender ladies, those delicate children, those brave hearts that had already endured so much, dared so much—should be sacrificed to the selfish idiocy of official routine, administered by imbeciles. It was a degrading cowardly fear of taking the slightest responsibility, when, by doing so, the lives of numbers of their fellow-countrymen might have been saved, that kept the major-general from sending aid; and, combined with this contemptible cowardice, was a still worse defect of character, a hard-hearted selfishness which prevented one man from sympathising with another.

Bad news somehow communicates itself. It seems to travel in the air, and to find its way into men's ears, even though untold.

It was the case in this instance. After about ten minutes' consultation with his friends, a consultation that consisted of little but invectives against the Mitterpore Red-Tapists, Dacres went outside for the purpose of seeing how he could best break the disastrous intelligence to the sepoys, and others who he doubted not were all anxiously looking out for news. He found it had preceded him: doubtless the kossid had told them something; at any rate, they had it all at their fingers' ends. There were no European soldiers come, and there were none coming. Like wildfire it spread from mouth to mouth; the sepoys ran out of their tents and huts, for many of them had been sheltered in the outhouses in the garden, and asked, 'What news?' They were answered by a sign, a waive of the hand, and a snap of the finger, very expressive, but not encouraging.

By the time Dacres got outside, they were all assembled in front of the door. One man came forward, a native officer of the irregulars, and spoke, respectfully enough, but less so than was his wont. 'His comrades,' he said, 'were all of one mind; they had stuck to the sahibs as long as they could, and defended them, and were ready to fight for them, and by this had lost caste among their own countrymen; but this they did not care for, as long as there was a hope of succour coming in the shape of European soldiers; but now that they found they had been deceived, that no assistance was coming, that the British rule was so effectually overturned that a general sahib had not a single soldier to save so many lives, it was useless for them any longer to keep up a show of resistance: the case was hopeless. Nothing could now save the few devoted victims of the mutiny. Why should they remain any longer, to share their certain and inevitable destruction? Besides, had they not been deceived? Had they not been promised reward, over and over again, if they remained faithful? Had they not been repeatedly assured that the mutiny was only a temporary and local check upon the power of the British government? Had not the kossid, who went at the imminent risk of his life all the way to Mitterpore and back again, been promised large rewards, of which not one rupee had reached him? What had happened that the word of British officers, till now scrupulously observed, had been broken, but that heaven had decreed that the rule should pass from them to others? They, too, must bow to the will of heaven, and leave the service of the English officers.'

After concluding his address, the man made a military salute and walked away. Nearly the whole of those assembled followed him, though many of them came and pressed the hands and knees of the officers they were deserting against their foreheads, and not a few had tears in their eyes.

'What, are you all going?' said Dacres. 'Wait till we see whether we do not get aid from Aurungabad. And yet no—I will hold out no further promises,' he added, speaking to himself and to those immediately around him. 'We have been basely betrayed by our own fellow-countrymen, basely deserted by them in our worst extremity: shall we expect these men to do more? We are deserted by all but God, but in Him will I trust while I have life.'

A few of the men remained behind. Among them was Asgar Ally, who had the minute before been seen holding commune with the deserters, to whom he was speaking in a very animated way, gesticulating and exhorting them to do something—what, Dacres could not hear. The men who remained, between fifteen and twenty, stepped forward and said—

'The sahib is our master: we will not leave him. Our lives are in the hands of God: if he dies, we will die too.'

Dacres took each man by the hand, and pressed it warmly. 'God bless you, my fine fellows!' he said—'I thank you all. Depend upon it, Alla will fight for those who fight for their honour and defend the right.'

'Did you see Asgar Ally?' said Thurston, whispering in Murray's ear. The officers were all standing in a small knot in the doorway while this scene was going on. 'He was persuading those deserters to go, I know he was.'

'Perhaps he was persuading them to stay.'

'Ah! you are blind and infatuated mortals,' replied Thurston. 'Infatuated! Infatuation is no word for it. With all their double-dyed treachery before your very eyes, you still trust a man with a black skin. For shame, Murray!'

'Why, how now?' said Dacres, who came up as he was speaking. 'This from you, Thurston? Why, you have slightly changed your mind of late. Not very long ago you were all for the black skin against the white skin. What about your moral influence, eh?'

'Moral influence, my dear sir? Why all that I have seen and suffered only goes to establish the soundness of my theory of moral influence. Had you tried a little more of the *moral influence* you despised so much, and not goaded these men to rebellion, we should have been spared all this. Your physical force, what does it amount to? Nothing. Had you depended on your moral influence in the days of your prosperity, you would have had it to depend upon now that physical support is withdrawn. But that has nothing to do with what I was saying, which is, that you do wrong to trust Asgar Ally.'

'What makes you think so?'

'Appearances.'

'Appearances made you think we had driven the brave sepoys to mutiny by our injustice and harshness—appearances were wrong.'

'Why were they wrong?'

Before any reply could be made to this by the man to whom it was addressed, an answer of a different kind, or rather, a practical comment upon Dacres' previous remarks, was made by the party of deserters, who had now reached the garden gate, and were leaving the premises in a crowd. About half a dozen of them remained behind their comrades, turned round, coolly levelled their muskets at the little knot of officers in the doorway, and fired into them. The bullets rattled about their heads, striking lintel and door-post, but not doing any damage. None of the officers stirred. Thurston, who was more exposed than the rest, never flinched.

'You are learning to stand fire pretty well, at any rate,' said Murray, laughing. 'These gentlemen have settled your argument for you; for my part, I shall go in.'

The sepoys, who, after remaining true to their officers under such tremendous temptation, and after refusing to join their comrades when they could have done so at first and share in all the advantages that had been reaped by those who had taken part in the rebellion in its first stage, and had now made such a dastardly attempt upon their officers, coolly shouldered their muskets and followed the rest.

As soon as Dacres got inside he met Mrs. Murray, who was in search of him. She was coming to the door when the volley of musketry frightened her, and she ran back for shelter.

'Do come and see poor Captain Stevens; he has sent for you,' she said.

Dacres immediately went to the sick man's room. There, standing by the bedside, he found Amy, and, to his surprise, Burleigh also. Amy was crying, and the tears were chasing one another down her cheeks rapidly. Burleigh was much affected, though he exhibited less outward signs of emotion.

'What was that firing?' asked Stevens, in a very faint whisper.

'Some rascally deserters giving us a volley just as they were going off.'

'What, have the men deserted?' said Burleigh.

'Yes, most of them.'

'No help from Mitterpore?'

'None whatever.'

'God help *you*,' said the sick man, with stress on the last word, and speaking in so low a voice that he could scarce make himself heard. 'Give me your hand, Dacres.'

He took it and pressed it. 'I am going from you,' he said, 'to join my darlings. Would that you could all go with me—now—as peacefully as I.'

All were silent: they spoke only with their tears.

'Keep it up to the last, Dacres—don't give in—strengthen the outer redoubt as much as you can. If they bring guns, you must send the ladies down below directly. And you, Amy——'

He took his sister's hand and gazed wistfully into her face. The state of utter desolation in which he was leaving her seemed to come vividly before him.

'Amy,' he said, after a pause and a struggle to suppress a sob, 'God will protect you. Take care of poor Georgy as long as you can. And you, Burleigh, look here. I know you love her, for you have told me so. There was one who was dearer to her than you, I know; but he is gone. Amy will be left utterly defenceless, utterly unprovided for, when I am gone too. I am, I was her guardian; to you I leave her, and if you get out of this you will know how to make her happy. Amy, dearest, give him your hand before I die; it will be a relief to me to know you are not left utterly unprotected.'

She looked up through her tears, first at her brother, and saw his agonised and anxious gaze, and then at Burleigh. Neither spoke, but she placed her hand in his, and felt really in the presence of death, and before God, his affianced wife.

'Now, Dacres, read to me. And, stay, do not go away any of you—join us.'

Dacres took up an old worn fragment of a church prayer-book, one of the few precious relics they had preserved, and read the prayers for the visitation of the sick. At times he was forced to stop, and the solemn silence of that chamber of death was broken by suppressed sobbing. Suddenly there was a sound of distant firing, volley after volley. Dacres read on calmly and impressively, though his voice trembled as he pronounced the words, so full of awful import to those present: 'And teach us who survive'—another distant volley—'in this and other like daily spectacles of mortality to see how frail and uncertain our own condition is, and'—another volley—'so to number our days that we may seriously apply our hearts to that holy and heavenly wisdom while we live here, which may in the end bring us to life everlasting.'

He rose from his knees—there was a great commotion down below—looked at Amy, touched Burleigh on the arm, and they left the two women with the dying man—

For men must work, and women must weep.

CHAPTER XLVII.

We left the Nawab endeavouring to comfort Leila under the tremendous blow which had reached her—from some unseen hand, as it appeared to him, ignorant as he was of what had passed. It was long before the second outburst of grief subsided, and still longer before she was sufficiently calm to speak in a connected way. At last, however, she recovered herself; and then followed a recital of what seemed to him a stranger tale than any he had heard related by the travelling storytellers that occasionally in Eastern lands unfold to wondering audiences the marvels of the Arabian nights, and similar compositions. I may spare the reader the tale, for it was simply a history of all that had taken place since first the Mirza had obtained entrance to her chamber in disguise. She concealed nothing. She acknowledged her fault, her imprudence, her guilty breach of etiquette in allowing a man, a stranger, to have free access to her apartments.

He sat silent, like one amazed, staring at the beautiful features of the fair narrator, lit up with a glow of enthusiasm, in a kind of wondering trance, playing nervously with the hilt of his dagger, at times drawing it partially from its sheath and then replacing it, as she dwelt with some lingering fondness, as he thought upon the too frequent visits of her mysterious guest. But when she came to the last part of her story, and her voice trembled and faltered, and her face was suffused with blushes, his calmness and stoicism left him; he leapt to his feet, and began pacing up and down the room, pausing every now and then in his walk, and turning and looking at her, at times almost fiercely, as if he wished to read, and to find out beforehand what she was about to reveal. Not a word did he speak till she had finished; he let her tell her story right through from beginning to end, without interrupting her once to ask a single question. She almost wished he had. It would have encouraged her to proceed, could she have known he trusted her, could she have got but one word of confidence and love. But not a sign did he vouchsafe: she was her own advocate, and he left her ample time to plead her cause. As she finished, she threw herself on her knees, and implored his pardon. He raised her and kissed her tenderly on the forehead.

'I forgive you, child, but you have done wrong; you have allowed yourself to be duped by this deceiver, this enchanter, this magician—for enchanter he must be, as by enchantment alone could he have so blinded my Leila's eyes to what was right and honourable. Now, tell me, where is he?'

'Alas, I know not! When I screamed and fainted I saw him no more. He doubtless fled, alarmed at my summoning assistance.'

'What was it he said?—that he would raise my men against me?'

'Yes, he threatened me with that. He swore that your life and my honour were in his hands, and he would have both. He swore he would stir up your men to revolt, as he has stirred up the British soldiers to revolt, and in the general confusion and disturbance he would ruin you and me too, and secure the destruction of those he hates above all living kind, the kaffir fugitives.'

'And you betrayed that fair girl to this devil's clutches! You, Leila, so good and pure yourself, you try to betray another of a different creed and race, and your husband's guest too, as pure as—by Alla—as pure as you are and as innocent. By heaven, if this is not a transformation, or the work of magic, I know not what is.'

Leila pressed her hands to her face; the burning tears forced their way between her fingers.

'I swear by heaven,' she said, making a violent effort to restrain herself, 'I was ignorant—utterly ignorant of his devices, of his intentions. I trusted him, fool that I was—I trusted him with my own honour. Should I have feared to trust him with that of this kaffir girl? Never till I saw his baseness, never till he himself threw off the mask, had I once thought of what his real intentions were. He had some strange power of fascination—some secret hidden art by which he could enslave those he fixed his desires on. And at the last, when his true character stood revealed to me, it was long, long before I could find strength to throw off this strange, mysterious, unseen fetter that he cast around me. His eye was upon me, and by its very glance he seemed to have the power of binding me down. I could not weep. I could not tear myself away, till long, long after I yearned to do so with my whole soul. At last he took his eye off me—he ceased suddenly to command, and turned to entreat: he besought, he implored my acquiescence in his guilty love, and then, then in one moment I felt free as air, and I tore myself from him; with one bound I leapt across the room, and spent all my remaining strength in that piercing call for help. It was that cry you heard, and that cry that drove him off.'

'And who were his accomplices? for it is impossible that he could come and go without the connivance of the servants and the guards.'

'Ah! I had forgotten; your words remind me. Now will I show you how I have been betrayed. Look here: you remember Sidi Gulzar bringing me this cup of sherbet, and how I just put it—only just put it—to my lips. Here it is. Now, see. Among the many wonderful mysteries in science I learnt from the lips of this minister of Eblis was the nature and use of poison, and their antidotes. See, I have a goodly store of them.'

She drew aside a curtain that concealed a recess in which a large-sized chest was standing. This she unlocked by a key that was attached to a gold chain round her neck. The chest was filled with bottles and jars of all kinds and sizes. The Nawab gazed in astonishment at all this paraphernalia of witchcraft as he thought them, and then looked at Leila to explain it. The very possession of so much knowledge and such wonderful apparatus seemed to raise her in his estimation; whether it increased his love for her, I know not.

'Now look,' she continued. 'Give me that goblet.' The Nawab brought it.

She selected one small phial from the number that filled the bottom of the chest. It contained a little white liquid. 'Now,' she said, 'if, as I suspect, this sherbet is poisoned, when I pour a drop of this liquid from the phial into it you will see a cloud-like substance forming in it, which will collect, and then gradually fall to the bottom of the glass.'

She poured a little of the sherbet from the silver cup into a small glass, and added a drop or two from the phial she had taken from the chest. The Nawab watched her. In a few seconds, indeed almost instantaneously, after the two liquids met, the cloud-like substance she had spoken of formed and settled at the bottom of the glass.

She looked at her husband.

'This poison,' she said, 'is so deadly, that the draught I should have taken, had I drunk that cupfull, would have been enough to destroy twenty such lives as mine. It must be he that instigated Sidi Gulzar to this dreadful crime, in the hope that I should not live to reveal all that he said to me.'

'Sidi Gulzar shall die for this—the villain—the traitor! I see. Give me the cup; we will send for him and tell him to drink it. If he knows what it is he will refuse, and then he shall be tortured till we get out of him all he does know.'

He went to the door, and, calling a servant, desired him to summon the chief eunuch instantly.

In a few minutes Sidi Gulzar stood before them, calm and self-possessed, without showing a trace of fear or emotion of any kind. He made a low salaam.

'Here, you have brought your mistress bad sherbet, Sidi Gulzar. How careless you are! As a punishment you shall be condemned to drink it, and then go and fetch some more.'

The eunuch smiled, made a salaam, and stretched out his hand for the goblet rather eagerly. As the Nawab handed it to him he managed to place his fingers awkwardly upon his master's, and then to slip them off to the handle of the cup, just as one might do in taking a glass or cup from another's hand in the dark or without looking. The Nawab moved his fingers as the other's touched them, never suspecting at the moment that any design lurked behind the apparently awkward little mistake. But it was done so well and so adroitly that between them both the goblet fell to the ground, and every drop of the sherbet was spilt on the floor, and this too in such a way that the Nawab felt he could not say it was the servant's fault. Whether done designedly or not, there was no more sherbet there to be drunk. The eunuch uttered an exclamation of disgust at his clumsiness and at the mess which the spilt sherbet had made upon the carpet, as he picked up the empty cup and took it away to get more.

The Nawab and Leila looked at each other; the former burst out laughing.

'By Alla, the rogue did it so cleverly I could not baulk him. What say you now, Leila—was it done by accident, or is he guilty of complicity? But I must go. Drink no more sherbet, Leila. I will have the eunuch seized and examined. What you have said to-night has made me anxious about my own affairs, and I must go and see that this cur does not carry out his threats and tamper with my men.'

The time that had elapsed during Leila's fainting fit and her subsequent narrative and the events that followed had brought in the dawn: the Eastern horizon was bright when the Nawab reached his own chamber. There he gave directions for having the chief eunuch seized and put in confinement in a place where he could hold no communication with anyone; and after sending for his most trustworthy deewans or counsellors he set about to turn over in his mind the probabilities of the Mirza being able to carry out his designs. What those designs were he fully understood. The Mirza had from the first time he became acquainted with him been an uncompromising foe to the British government and a staunch supporter of the upstart king of Delhi. He saw that now it was a matter of choice merely between rebellion against the British government or a dangerous and doubtful struggle for his own safety. The temper of his men he knew was such that a spark would fire the train. That spark the Mirza would strike—there was no doubt of it. They only wanted a leader such as he—a bold, daring, enterprising spirit—to lead the way, and they were all willing enough to follow. The example set by the British native troops was one only too likely to be followed. He knew, as he had told Mr. Dacres often, that if he could succeed in restraining his men, in keeping them to their allegiance for a few days, it was all he could do: if in that time the succour expected from Mitterpore arrived, they might undoubtedly tide over the crisis—they would be saved.

Supported by alliance with the British government, and by the bayonets of British soldiers, he would be secure enough. Once on the winning side, once on the side of the strongest, there was no doubt about the allegiance of the majority. But should there be any delay in sending the troops from Mitterpore, or should any unforeseen event occur to heighten the excitement that still prevailed among the men, or should any one individual of more energy than the rest raise the standard of revolt, there was no room for any doubt as to the result. The Nawab would have either to take the lead in the movement, by putting himself at the head of the insurgents and leading them against the British (for if he did that his popularity would remain unimpaired), or he might make an ineffectual struggle against thousands, and perish with the small band of Englishmen whose lives were already hanging by a thread.

Then there was Doonghur Rao. A ray of hope came from that quarter. Hitherto he had done, unintentionally no doubt, the greatest service to the cause of the British interests and the Nawab, by keeping the soldiery employed and the country in a ferment. He *might* keep them so engaged till things took a favourable turn. But should his men obtain a victory over Doonghur Rao, which was a finale to the affair he hourly expected to hear of, then, flushed with success, they would only be the more bent on carrying out their treasonable designs. Should Doonghur Rao prove victorious, the bulk of the soldiers would return to Islamabad in disorder and excitement, and in that case, too, mutiny was the most likely thing for them to turn their hands to. That the two contending parties should coalesce and direct their united efforts to one object, namely, the support of the rebels, the Nawab never for a moment dreamed. It may be imagined, therefore, what was his consternation and horror when the tidings reached him, as they did that evening, that Doonghur Rao's troops had joined his own, and that the two parties had united and hoisted the green flag, and were in full march upon Islamabad, bent on securing the acknowledgment of the Nawab to the paramount power of the reigning scion of the house of Timour, or——the alternative was not a pleasant one.

The whole of the day was spent by the Nawab in vain attempts to keep up appearances. Very few, if any, of the people about him could be trusted; even those on whom he reposed most confidence and pretended really to rely, had long ago, he well knew, made up their minds how they should behave in the crisis which must come sooner or later. With the exception of the troops in camp not a soul had as yet committed himself openly by word or deed to the rebellion; yet the Nawab knew as well as if they had told him what course they intended to pursue, provided the reinforcements from Mitterpore never came. All hinged upon that: and when next day the kossid's return and the unsuccessful issue of his mission was noised abroad, as it was with the speed of lightning, the conflagration broke out at once. It was heightened by the arrival of the whole of the mutineers, as I may now call them, from the Kooria hills. They marched up with colours flying and drums beating to the very walls of the palace, and pitched their camp outside. The inhabitants of the city flocked out in crowds to meet them, and the greatest possible excitement reigned everywhere. Old Doonghur Rao was a great centre of attraction; hundreds, aye thousands, hastened to gaze at him. Hussain Khan, who was called himself Sipah Salar, or Commander-in-Chief, was quite jealous of the attention shown to his late rival.

It was now absolutely necessary for the Nawab to decide what course he should pursue. As yet he had been treated with nothing but respect; but when he sent out (for form's sake he was obliged to take some notice of it) to enquire who it was that without permission had marched his troops up to the very palace walls and encamped outside them, answer was sent that the chiefs were preparing to wait on his highness, if his highness would graciously accept the deputation. He sent back word he would be delighted to receive them, and gave orders for the immediate preparation of the Dewan-i-amm, or public hall of audience.

He had a few minutes only to himself. He sat down and wrote a letter to Mr. Dacres, as follows:—

'After compliments, the Nawab of Islamabad to his trusty friend and counsellor Dacres, Sahib Bahadoor, commissioner of the British government for the district of Islamabad—

'We are fallen on evil times. Alla has poured out the cup of wrath on his creatures: short space has this well-wisher of the British government for writing, and short space for reflection. Surrounded by violent men, as the stars in heaven for multitude, who are ready to take the life of this well-wisher, unless he consents to put himself at their head, and lead them on in rebellion against the British government, and seeing that no alternative is open but either to take the post offered to him, in which, no doubt, he will be enabled by the blessing of Alla to ward off many blows and disasters from his friend, or to place his neck under the ruthless sword of the executioner (not that he values in the least degree, even to a hair, his own vile life, but is only anxious to secure his friends), this well-wisher has resolved to take in the hand of necessity the sword of duplicity, and writes to warn his friend that the mask of deceit is put on at the bidding of destiny. What need of more?—written words are dangerous.'

Having finished this scrawl, he sent for two of his ministers, and desired them to certify at the foot of the document, which he did not permit them to read, that it was penned and signed by him on such a date, noting the day and hour. He then dismissed them, and hurried to Leila's apartments, where, without danger of being overlooked, he concealed the note, squeezed up into the smallest possible compass, in the folds of his turban.

I will not detain the reader by describing the interview between the Nawab and Leila. It was brief; he had a presentiment of coming trouble, and wished, before he parted from her, perhaps for ever, to repeat and to hear again from her lips those vows of constancy and words of love they had often interchanged. As he left her, after a long embrace, he held out his hand, and pointed to a ring on his forefinger.

'Look, Leila,' he said. 'You see this ring—this one, the opal set in emeralds. If evil befall me, and Alla wills that we meet the worst, and Azrael's approach can no longer be warded off by mortal means, you will receive from me this ring—a silent messenger of sorrow and of death, but not of dishonour. By the time it reaches you I shall have fallen; for I will not send it till the last. When I am gone you are at the mercy of the destroyer—you understand me? You will not survive me to live dishonoured and disgraced, the slave to minister to the passion of this cursed son of Satan?'

She intimated through her tears her assent, and with another embrace they parted.

After completing a few additions to his toilet, the Nawab summoned his suite to accompany him to the hall of audience. As he went along the gallery leading from his own room to the lower part of the palace, he passed an open window looking down on the plain on which the camp was pitched. Here, in a most conspicuous part of the field, he saw his own tents erected, with a green flag at the summit of a tall flagstaff in front.

'By whose orders were my tents pitched?' he asked.

'By the commander-in-chief's,' was the reply.

He said no more, but continued his way. As he reached the bottom of the flight of steps leading from the upper to the lower story, he bethought himself of the imprisoned eunuch, whom he had totally forgotten in the press of business, and the multitude of anxieties that had filled his mind for the last forty-eight hours. It was too late then to go and see him, so he contented himself with directing one of his servants to give orders that the chief eunuch, who was confined in one of the turrets of the palace, should be supplied with food, mentally resolving that, as soon as the very disagreeable and important business he had on hand was transacted, he would proceed to the examination of the prisoner. The servant received the order, but much preferred going with the rest to witness the grand ceremony in the hall of audience, and thought the necessary instructions about so insignificant a matter as the eunuch's food could be given as well after as before the durbar.

CHAPTER XLVIII.

The hall was full to overflowing long before the Nawab reached it. He did not enter, however, at the door by which the chiefs and their retainers gained admission, but by a private entrance communicating with his own apartment, that opened out on to the dais or raised platform, elevated about six inches from the floor of the hall itself, on which the Nawab and the dignitaries and chief men who came to transact business at the public durbars were accustomed to seat themselves, in distinction from the common herd who filled the lower part of the spacious room.

No sooner had the Nawab entered, and the door was closed behind him, than he found himself surrounded by a very strong body of fierce-looking barbarians, clad in no uniform like his own soldiers, but all well armed, their matchlocks in their hands, and matches lighted.

He glanced round at the savage features of the semi-barbarous warriors, and then somewhat nervously turned his eye in the direction of the crowd. Here he saw all strange faces. There were none of his own retainers, none of his own sepoys: the large hall was quite full of armed men; they were the ruffian followers of Doonghur Rao. From the more distant part of the hall, the Nawab, now really feeling, though without exhibiting, the least alarm, turned his eye upon the group that lined the dais; they were native officers and chiefs, and they all stood with their shields slung on their shoulders, and their swords drawn in their hands, the points resting on the ground.

Immediately in front stood old Doonghur Rao, the (usually) grey hair on his face, his whiskers and moustache, and the beard parted in the centre and under the chin and stretching out horizontally from his face to right and left, all dyed jet black, as if he was a young man of five and twenty. The old robber had an unpleasant twinkle in his little black eyes, and a smile about the corners of his mouth, as if he was thoroughly enjoying something that he kept, however, to himself. Next to him stood Hussain Khan, a fine-looking Mahometan gentleman of Rohilcund, with the fair complexion and Jewish features characteristic of the descendants of the Afghan conquerors of that fertile province. He was a complete contrast to the rough burly-looking robber chief that stood next to him; his dress, that of an Afghan of high rank, bedizened with gold tinsel, which Asiatics are so fond of, was faultless of its kind, though it would have suited a courtier better than a soldier. A silver-mounted pistol was stuck showily in his waistband; and the scabbard of his sword, which hung resting on the ground, was a mass of gold. On the right and left stood a dozen or so of the chiefs and officers, descending by regular gradation from the higher to the lower ranks, and the circle was completed by the armed followers of Doonghur Rao.

Had the Nawab any doubts or misgivings as to his position, and the intention of those who now almost undisguisedly acted as his captors, they were soon resolved into certainty, for Hussain Khan stepped forward, and after a formal military salute put a written paper into the Nawab's hands, and desired him, in a tone respectful but firm, almost commanding, to advance to the edge of the dais and read it out, adding that he had permission to peruse it first.

The Nawab took the paper with as much dignity as he could assume, and read it.

Hussain Khan gave him time to master its

contents, and to ponder on them too; but seeing that the Nawab hesitated to comply with his demand, he made a sign to the armed ruffians that surrounded him: they, in obedience to the intimation given, coolly raised their matchlocks and began blowing up the matches preparatory to firing.

The Nawab pretended not to notice this ominous movement, though we may be sure he saw and understood it; and, finding escape absolutely hopeless, he signified his intention of reading aloud the paper.

At a second sign from Hussain Khan, the row of chiefs who lined the dais opened and allowed the Nawab to approach to the very edge, where, after again looking round on the multitude assembled before him, he read with a loud, clear, and distinct voice as follows:—

'Be it known throughout Islam, and let it be especially promulgated in the city and territory of Islamabad, that the servant of the Most High God, and humble attendant at the threshold of the Sovereign, the Light of Islam, the Emperor of Hindustan, has thrown aside the cloak of allegiance to the infidels, whom hitherto, by the decree of destiny, and the prevalence of the powers of evil, he has been necessitated to serve, and has sent to the footstool of the King of kings his humble declaration of feudal obedience, and has raised in the plain of brave intentions the standard of the Mahometan faith, round which all faithful and true servants of God and the Prophet, and all our faithful and well-meaning Hindoo subjects and brethren, chiefs, rajahs, raeeses, and soldiers, are called upon to rally and assemble this day, in order that, imploring the aid of heaven and the blessing of the Prophet on our laudable endeavours, we may set our hands to the extermination of the infidel from the earth in these territories assigned to us by the Most High.

'And to our Hindoo fellow-soldiers and subjects who join with us in this praiseworthy design, we hereby promise to extend to them the right hand of amity and good-will, and to treat them on all occasions as if they were the servants and followers of the Prophet. While every man, Hindoo and Mahometan, shall be allowed to follow his own religion, all shall equally share in the good government of the country, and the offices of state, and the conduct of the army. In token hereof, we do now appoint our trusty ally and friend Doonghur Rao a Mansabdar of 10,000, and his chiefs, Anar Singh, Buldeo Singh, Sita Ram, Kasi Rao, and Dhiraj Singh, Mansabdars of 5,000. Our well-beloved and trusty Hussain Khan Bahadoor, we appoint Commander-in-Chief

Sipah Salar) of our own forces, and we decree to him a tenth of all the spoil taken by our forces from the infidel, and we appoint him Mansabdar of 10,000, and his chiefs and officers, Emmam Khan, Sirbuland Khan, Shekh Mahrab-ood-deen, Peer Khan, and Tegh Ally Khan, we appoint colonels of our regiments, and Mansabdars each of 1,000, and a title to one-third of the spoil taken from the infidels.

'This is written and proclaimed by this servant of God, this fourteenth day of Zilhuz, in the year of the Hegira 1277.'

This ceremony having been completed, the Nawab was conducted in state, and with all possible outward signs of respect, to his seat on the back of the dais, where he remained while the officers mentioned in his proclamation brought 'nazurs' or presents, consisting of pieces of money, jewels, &c. &c., on the occasion of their appointment. After this was over, various papers containing different orders and instructions were brought to him for signature. They related entirely to details connected with furnishing supplies for the army, collection of revenue, &c. &c. This occupied some time; when it was over, the Nawab was led, still a prisoner in reality, though surrounded with all the externals of royalty, to the court-yard of his palace. Here his horse, fully caparisoned, awaited him: he mounted, his faithful guard or escort surrounded him, and so the cortége rode through the city down to the camp on the plain beyond, the people assembling in crowds in the streets and roads to see him pass, and shouting out their acclamations as he went along. At his tent he dismounted, and, as he entered, volleys of musketry were fired in honour of the event; and this occasioned the report heard at the Sudder Ameen's house, and interrupted the solemn duties in which the party were there engaged around the bed of death.

CHAPTER XLIX.

The means that had been taken for the defence of Meer Ally Moorad's house were the best that could have been devised or carried out under the circumstances, and with the slender resources at the disposal of the small garrison. Fortunately, they were all pretty well completed before the desertion of the larger portion of the sepoys, so that they had the advantage of their manual labour, at any rate.

The house itself was a double-storied one, built of stone and masonry, with a flat roof surrounded by a balustrade, also of masonry, but erected only for ornament, and, therefore, neither massive nor durable. The interstices between these balustrades were filled in with bricks made of mud and baked in the sun, apertures being left at stated intervals for musketry. The same plan was carried out with the windows and doors, though not to such an extent as to exclude altogether air and light. The most important, however, of all the defences were those which would have to be held before the house itself was reached by an enemy, and which were built in such a way as to afford a very formidable obstacle to any body of men who should attempt to carry the place by storm. The rear of the house was pretty well protected by a massive wall of mud, surmounted by a parapet, behind which men could easily conceal themselves, and fire through the loopholes in the battlements, without the smallest danger of being hit themselves from the outside. The present house had been erected by the father of the late owner, on an estate conferred upon him for eminent services to the British government. The old fort he had pulled down, all except a portion of the wall, which was left standing, either from caprice, or on the same principle that we throw an old shoe after a new married couple for good luck. Anyhow, there the wall stood, and, as it turned out, was of most invaluable service to the party of refugees that were driven, by the strange combination of circumstances, to take shelter behind it. The part of the house that required the most engineering skill and labour to render it secure was the front. Here there was but one door. To protect this two redoubts had been thrown up, under Stevens's direction, opposite the two corners of the house, about one hundred yards from the walls. These redoubts were connected with the house by a covered way, so that the defenders, when driven out at the last extremity, could effect their escape with tolerable safety. The redoubts, of course, were very small miniature affairs altogether compared to what redoubts generally are, but they were suited to the size of the garrison, and, as far as they went, perfect productions of engineering skill. Between the two redoubts a ditch had been dug, and ramparts thrown up, so as to connect the two and afford covered communication, rather than for any defensive purposes, the redoubts themselves affording all the defence that was required, as it would be impossible for an attacking party to storm the house itself till they had possession of these outworks. On the two flanks of the house, where there were no doors to defend, the walls were protected by parallel rows of outhouses, all built of mud. These outhouses were thrown down, and their débris arranged in such a manner as to allow a man to stand and fire over the top, or through the loopholes that had, in some places only, been made. These outhouses afforded no very great protection, but they were easily held, and the approach to them was enfiladed from the wall of the fortification behind, as well as from the rear face of the front redoubts. I have only further to state that all the trees in the gardens had been cut away, all the shrubs and underwood removed, and nothing within a mile left that could afford cover to an approaching enemy.

In addition to this, however, some pains had been bestowed upon erecting a defence in front of the door of the tomb, with which the house communicated by the subterraneous passage before described.

In carrying out this, no resort had ever been made to the passage as a means of communication. Its very existence was kept a dead secret by all who knew of it from all who did not; the working parties who went daily to carry out the operations at the tomb, went and came back by the ordinary road round the house. The defence consisted of simple redoubts opposite each door—the best method of protection that can possibly be resorted to where the labour of the garrison requires to be economised.

It was not long before our friends' defences had to be tested rather rudely.

On the evening of the day on which the Nawab had, under pressure, assumed the mock powers of an independent prince, a grand review of the whole troops was ordered, and he was requested—I may as well say ordered—to attend in all the pomp and state that could be mustered. The following morning was fixed for the opening of operations against the infidels, and the review was intended as a grand military spectacle, calculated, by the glitter and parade of war, to rouse the enthusiasm of the multitude of warriors that were gathered together to something like fighting pitch.

At the appointed hour, preceded by mounted trumpeters blowing their trumpets, and other musicians beating the monotonous kettle-drum, the emblem of sovereignty, followed by the umbrella-bearer, the other emblem of royal dignity in this land of state and ceremony, the Nawab rode, on a richly-caparisoned prancing horse, to the spot where the whole force was drawn up in line. At a distance, indeed, it looked imposing; and perhaps the Nawab might have been pardoned if his breast did beat at the thought of the glorious position Fate had suddenly thrust him into. Unfortunately for his friends, or his ambition, he felt that, amid all this splendour, and surrounded with all these externals of majesty and power, he was after all but a captive and a slave. There had been, however, not a moment, since he first took the part assigned to him and read out the proclamation of rebellion as his own, that he had met with the slightest shadow of disrespect. On that score, at any rate, he had nothing to complain of.

I need not describe all the strange evolutions and manœuvres that were performed by this gallant army for the inspection of their chiefs. They marched this way and that, ran, charged, fired, retreated, advanced, &c. &c., over and over again. The firing, indeed, was an important part of the day's proceedings, and one that did more than anything else to answer the end and object of the spectacle, viz. to get up the courage of the soldiers to fighting point; for on the morrow they were likely to have such fighting as they never before experienced, seeing that they were about to contend with the 'Devils of the West,' as the Chinese call us, even though, reckoned in numbers, there were certainly more than a hundred to one in proportion to those same 'devils.' One thing had attracted the Nawab's notice very much. It was this:

During the review he sat on his horse by the side of the green flag that was stuck in the ground at one point of the field, by which the troops first marched in review order, with the exception of Doonghur Rao's men, who did not attempt the more difficult movements of the military programme. The Nawab was attended by his usual escort, or a guard of honour, as he was told to consider it, and by several of the chiefs and officers besides, among whom were personages of no less importance than Hussain Khan and Doonghur Rao themselves. That these notables should remain inactive the Nawab thought very strange: it did not strike him that, in the compact between the two rebel chiefs, there was one insuperable obstacle at the outset, which was no other than this—that Hussain Khan's men would not submit to be commanded by Doonghur Rao, nor did Doonghur Rao's followers deem it consistent with their dignity to be commanded by Hussain Khan. Fortunately for the designs of the ambitious leaders, there was no need of bringing this question to issue. The Nawab observed that all the evolutions of the troops were directed and controlled by a horseman of noble bearing and great stature, conspicuous among all the chiefs and the retinue that surrounded him by the magnificence of his dress, the size of his steed and its gaudy caparisons, and the graceful yet soldier-like seat of the rider. He wore a coat of polished mail that glittered like a mirror in the afternoon sun: a turban, with a bunch of eagle feathers in it, adorned his head, and over his shoulder and across his breast he wore a green scarf.

'Pray,' said the Nawab, as soon as the conclusion of the review and the cessation of firing allowed him to speak with any chance of being heard—addressing Hussain Khan—'who is yon chief I see directing all the movements of the troops? He sits on his horse right well.'

'May it please your highness,' said Hussain Khan, 'it is the renowned champion of Islam, sent from heaven to lead the soldiers of the Prophet to victory against the Nazarenes.'

'I saw him not at the durbar.'

'No, your highness; he was then engaged in prayer and holy communion with the angel Gabriel.'

'Who and what is he?' again asked the Nawab, with an expression of some disdain, as if he half thought the other was trifling with him.

'We hardly know. Some call him the Imam Mehndi, and others say he is the Prophet Esa reappeared on earth, as prophesied in the holy book, at the latter days: others say he is the brother of the angel Gabriel; and others, the ignorant and common herd, call him the Mirza.'

The Nawab's horse suddenly reared, curvetted, and finally made a pirouette on its hind legs. His rider must have twisted the bit fiercely in its mouth, or dug his spurs into its sides, or otherwise vented his emotion on the harmless but spirited animal, to make it so restive. With pale face, and lips livid as if from rage, the Nawab spoke, as soon as his horse was quiet:

'Will you summon the Mirza to my presence? Angel or devil, while he commands my troops it is fit he present his nuzzur.'

This assumption and active exercise of the authority they had pressed the Nawab to take, and tried to make him believe belonged to him, rather pleased Hussain Khan than otherwise. He bowed low, and sent an aide-de-camp to the chief, with a message saying that the Nawab had expressed a wish to see him.

Nothing occurred to break the silence till the aide-de-camp had ridden across the field to the chief, delivered his message, and returned, following behind the Mirza at a respectful distance. The Nawab sat like a statue on his horse, watching the officer take the message, and the two returning. Hussain Khan also sat without speaking; so did the other officers and leaders, who formed a semicircle round their new sovereign.

As the Mirza rode up, the Nawab's face became paler and paler; still he sat motionless, with his eyes fixed steadily on the approaching horseman. He rode up so close that their horses' heads almost touched each other; he then made a deep obeisance, or salaam, bending forward to the saddle-bow. The events I attempt to describe were momentary and simultaneous. As the Mirza rose to an erect position on his saddle, the Nawab, who had had his eyes steadily on him all the while, had drawn his pistol, and before anyone present had time to do more than notice the movement, he fired it in the Mirza's face. The attendant chiefs were at first too much horrified and thunderstruck to speak, but a kind of low suppressed murmur of horror and surprise escaped them. It was all over in a moment. As the smoke cleared off directly after the pistol had been fired, the Mirza was seen sitting on his horse unharmed, and smiling blandly: he held out his left arm at full length, and between his finger and thumb, extended so that all might see it, was the bullet.

The Nawab dashed his pistol angrily to the earth, and drew his sword.

'Alla Akbar, God is great!' exclaimed the

whole assemblage with one voice when they saw the miracle.

'Alla Akbar, God is great!' repeated the crowd of foot-soldiers and attendants, at the same time throwing themselves on their faces to the ground in adoration.

'Cut down the infidel!' cried two or three of the mounted chiefs, riding at the same moment down upon the Nawab and brandishing their naked swords.

Hussain Khan spurred his horse and got in between the indignant avengers of the Mirza and their intended victim.

'Spare violence,' he called out with dignity and a tone of command, holding out his hand in a forbidding and menacing attitude at the same time. 'Do no violence; his highness has acted thus merely to show to you all in public the invincible nature of the messenger and leader whom heaven hath sent to guide us to victory. By this miracle, which ye could not else have witnessed, hath it been proved that this our true leader is a prophet, the favoured of Alla, protected by the invisible shield of the angel Gabriel. Alla Akbar, God is great! who can thus preserve and distinguish his chosen ones.'

'Hussain Khan has spoken well,' said the

Nawab, sheathing his sword, and disguising as much as possible his real feelings of chagrin, hatred, and disgust. 'Now let the troops return to camp, and we will retire, for it is the hour of evening prayer.' With these words, and bowing haughtily to the assembled chiefs, he rode slowly away, followed by his escort.

'Why did you save the cursed fool's life?' said Doonghur Rao to Hussain Khan, as they rode off the ground together.

'Because,' replied he, as a smile played about the corner of his mouth, 'it can be undone at any time that; but matters are not settled yet, and it may be that after all the English infidels get the day. The Nawab stands high with them.'

A crowd had gathered round the Mirza by this time, and it seemed as if his prophetic character was not averse to a little vulgar popularity. He had been fully prepared for the Nawab's firing at him the first moment they met. The feat which looked like a miracle in the eyes of all the beholders was one of the most common of those performed nightly before large audiences in different conjuring saloons in Europe. The Nawab might load his pistol twenty times a day; twenty times a day the ball would be withdrawn or the loaded weapons exchanged for unloaded ones. With spies and accomplices and assistants everywhere, even in the Nawab's bed-chamber, the Mirza was all-powerful. At any rate it formed no part of his plans to be shot just yet, though it served to mystify the people; and expecting to be shot at with a pistol loaded with blank charge, he took care to have a bullet loose about his person available at any moment. To astonish still more the gaping crowd, he flourished the bullet about in his hand, and finally swallowed it. Then leaning forward he put his hand down to his horse's mouth and drew the bullet slowly out of the animal's nostril.

'Alla Akbar, God is great!' again roared the multitude, and went away with the firm belief that they had been in the company of the angel Gabriel, or at any rate his brother.

CHAPTER L.

THANKS to Asgar Ally's accurate information, the party in Meer Ally Moorad's house were kept fully aware of nearly all that passed in the Nawab's camp, and at his warning they now took measures to resist a general attack the following morning. The grand spectacle of the review and the noise and bluster of so much gunpowder was supposed to have aroused the enthusiasm of the soldiers to the necessary height, and it was resolved in the counsels of the chiefs, though as yet a secret to the Nawab, to march that night, and make the attack on the house at dawn the following day.

The party that were there to be assailed was well prepared. Poor Stevens had been buried alongside of his wife and child, and Amy, now left in sole charge of little Georgy, felt as if the greatest mercy heaven could show them both would be to send them by one bullet to join the dear ones who had so recently departed from the scenes of strife and misery that now encompassed them. She was beside herself with grief. She tried to read: even the pages of holy writ and the deep feeling of the Psalmist, poured forth in the words of inspired song, failed to arrest her attention. She tried to pray, but could not: she tried to weep, the tears would not flow. Silent and in despair, with her long hair drooping over her to the ground, she sat upon a low stool by the bedside, now empty, her hands pressed against her throbbing temples and aching eye-balls, the picture of despair and grief. Georgy, inured to the hardships of their present mode of life in some measure, and all unconscious of the terrible bereavement that had befallen him, which he could not realise, was playing with the other children; he was dirty, his face unwashed, his long hair matted, tangled, and uncombed, his clothes half torn off his back with romping; he would let no one but Amy touch him; if any of the other ladies went to him and tried to induce him to let them wash his hands and face and brush his hair, he shook off their gentle grasp angrily, and said that he would not have it done till his mama came to do it for him. Rather than force him into a roar, and depressed and half heart-broken themselves, the poor things left him alone. What did it matter now, a little dirt about a child's hands and face? All day long Amy sat there in the same position; no one thought of disturbing her. The gentlemen were all engaged in their preparations for defence—the ladies in assisting them: and Amy sat alone. It was not till late, till dark, that Georgy, being apparently induced by hunger to find out some protector or other, sought his way to the chamber lately occupied by his father and mother. He found it at last, all alone, and went in. Amy was roused from her stupor of despair by feeling a child's touch upon her hand. 'Aunty,' said a little voice, 'I am hungry.'

The simple allusion to such a common want, and that in the midst of the stunning blow of distress that had utterly broken down her spirits, aroused her to the realities of life. She clasped the child to her heart, and burst into a passionate flood of weeping. That timely safety-valve of nature had saved her reason. She got Georgy some food, and then washed his face and combed his hair; and as it was late, she heard him say his prayers, and then laid him down beside her in his bed, and fell asleep with his head resting on her arm; nor did she awake till started from her slumber by a heavy volley of musketry almost close at hand.

Though short in men, our friends were

remarkably well supplied with arms and ammunition, thanks to the stores laid up in the magazine below the house. Each man consequently provided himself with three muskets; and as they were pretty well resolved to retain their fire till they could deliver it with effect, they reckoned, and not unreasonably, that they had each the lives of three of their enemies at their disposal. There were altogether seventeen Englishmen and thirteen native sepoys, thirty in all. These were disposed in the most advantageous manner possible about the defences. Murray, with ten others, manned the two redoubts; Dacres took charge of the rear post with the flank defences, along and upon which the rest of the small party were stationed, with the exception of three officers and six sepoys who took post on the top of the house.

The final arrangements were scarce completed before the day dawned. With flags flying and drums beating, on came the attacking party. The Mirza rode in front, accompanied by a trooper bearing aloft a green flag on the end of a long bamboo; and behind him marched, in rather tumultuous array, the whole force. As they neared the post they were intending to storm, and where they expected opposition, what was their astonishment to see it totally deserted! Defences there were, it was true, but not a living soul was to be seen about the place. The warriors grew bold in proportion as their chance of finding an enemy disappeared. Whether the Mirza was led away with his enthusiasm, or whether, being aware of the existence of the secret passage, he had taken for granted that they had all retired there, and wanted to secure the approach, I know not; but he certainly led on his men in a most daring helter-skelter fashion. They approached nearer and nearer; still not a sign of a living creature was there. Up they came to within ten paces of the two redoubts. Then suddenly their course was arrested. At a given signal, as one man, the garrison of the redoubt fired without showing themselves. The nine-pounder mounted on the right redoubt gave out a dose of grape that did terrible execution at that distance, while every musket-shot brought down a man; but the Mirza was untouched. A second volley followed; again one man fell to each shot. Before the third reached them, they were flying pell-mell in the utmost possible confusion to the rear, treading upon one another's heels, and trampling under foot every unfortunate that stumbled. They had a good way to run before they got out of fire; meantime from every loophole where there was a man posted in any part of the defences except the left flank and left rear, from which no shots could be fired on the attacking or retreating party, the leaden messengers sped on their errand of death. As fast as they could lay down one musket and take up another—as fast as they could reload their pieces—did they keep up this deadly discharge; nor did they cease till the whole force had placed too great a distance between themselves and the vigorous garrison for the muskets of the defenders to reach them.

The rebels showed no disposition to renew the attack so inauspiciously begun, but contented themselves with pitching their camp just out of reach of the fire from the garrison. The defenders remained all day at their post, though they were exposed to the fury of the sun, tempered a good deal, however, by clouds which came up early in the morning, and ended in a protracted shower of rain which commenced at mid-day and continued during the afternoon.

The course which the rebel troops had taken in their attack was the one which had been recommended to them by Asgar Ally, who until now had passed himself off in the rebel camp as a spy engaged in their interests, just as he was trusted in the English garrison in the opposite character; and it was owing to his declared conviction to Murray and Dacres that the enemy would attack from that side, which had led those officers to make their arrangements with a view to meeting them so effectually there. The result had been eminently successful, but it was no longer possible for Asgar Ally to venture beyond the defences as heretofore in search of information. Nor was there anyone else to undertake the dangerous duty. The little garrison were therefore dependent on their eyes, and one telescope belonging to Mr. Dacres, for information regarding the movements of their enemies whom they carefully watched.

It soon became evident that their plan was to erect a battery, or a line of batteries, supplied with heavy guns. They could see workmen busily engaged in digging trenches, and heaping up the earth for parapets; and before dark more than one heavy piece of ordnance had been dragged down by bullocks and put into position. They did not, however, open fire. The day passed slowly and with anxiety, from which the shades of evening drawing on brought no relief.

CHAPTER LI.

THE monotonous duty of watching the movements of the enemy was relieved, about dusk, by the unexpected arrival of a spy, who, coming in the usual disguise of one of the sepoys from the enemy's camp, was as near as possible shot from the front redoubt. He made his mission, however, known in time, and was taken to Mr. Dacres. He came from the army head-quarters camp, and brought another secret missive from Sir Marmaduke Mastodon, which he carried, as did the other messengers, sewn in the leather of his shoe. Dacres opened it eagerly and read:—

'*To the Commissioner of Islamabad.*

'No news from below; all communication cut off: we do not know how matters are progressing with you, but fear the worst. All well here: the siege, a matter of time merely; we await reinforcements. Troops tolerably healthy; a good deal of cholera. There is a dangerous character abroad somewhere in your neighbourhood, about whom I wrote once before, but received no answer; am doubtful therefore if my messenger reached. I have in my possession a number of documents written in English and Persian, and signed by one Thurston, purporting to be addressed to the King of Delhi, and calling on him to rise, and all the sepoys, &c., to join; and that in doing so they will be supported by a large and powerful party in England, hostile to E. I. C., and anxious to ruin it at any cost by means of a general insurrection in this country.

'If you can catch the author, take care of him: don't hang him unless there is chance of his escape, but do not let him get away. Copies of this have been sent to other commissioners.

'P. S.—I leave this for Aurungabad to-night, with powers of special commissioner: from thence I shall proceed to any district that, from the accounts I receive, seem most to require assistance and looking after. I may come your way.'

Dacres read out this despatch, all except the part relating to Thurston, which indeed was the principal portion of the whole, to most of the officers of the garrison, who had assembled in the garden as soon as it had become bruited abroad that a kossid had come in; but, anxious to discuss the subject with Murray alone, he took him aside, and communicated the whole contents of the letter as they walked away together.

'Now, what do you say, Murray?' asked Dacres of his companion. 'Don't you think we had better have a court-martial or some enquiry upon this fellow? Is it safe to let him be going about at large?'

'My dear fellow, is it possible you really place any dependence on such a cock-and-bull story? Does it look probable? Here he is working and fighting like the rest of us: how can he be such a traitor, such a despicable wretch as Mastodon makes out? Depend on it, there is some infernal plot at the bottom of this, which we shall find out—if we ever get out of this hobble. These politicals are always the first to be hoodwinked and humbugged—they are the "curse of the country."'

'But you know Mastodon well enough: he is not like Sir Charles Napier's "sharp boys, who can speak Persian;" he is not the man to send a spy such a journey with a despatch sewn up in his shoe, and to give him a large reward, all for a mare's nest. Besides, do you not recollect the tenor of his conversation with me, the night of the mutiny? Why, he called these d——d traitors, these incarnate fiends—he called them "poor fellows," and said they were quite right to do what they had done. Then, by Jove, sir! he went to them—he went bang into their camp!'——

'Where he was as nearly as possible roasted alive for his folly.'

'So he said.'

'And so did not Asgar Ally, your "faithful and true," say, too?'

'Yes, indeed, Asgar Ally did say so; but I can't help thinking it was a plot.'

'A plot!—what, then, you distrust Asgar Ally after all!'——

'Not at all—not in the least. By a plot, I mean some plot of this deep designing villain and his friends, to take us all in. As for no European being such an abandoned villain as to take part with these murderous wretches, why there is one in camp yonder, at this moment, directing all their operations—and he seems the most bloodthirsty of all. Besides, why is Thurston always so hot against Asgar Ally—why is he always trying to poison our minds against him, and trying to make us distrust and drive the man from us, when he is the most valuable ally?'

'He declares he distrusts him, and that he is only here to betray us,' said Murray; 'and he thinks it is his duty to open our eyes to the man's real character.'

'And this is what I cannot bear in the conceited brute, just fresh from home, a mere griff (if he is just from home): he talks and lectures us in his insufferable conceit, as if he knew anything about the natives or about the country; he talks as if he had been in the service all his life, and understood the subject thoroughly. I declare it is sickening, sometimes to hear the fellow gabble.'

'My dear Dacres,' said Murray, quite amused at his friend's warmth, 'don't let your feelings carry you beyond the bounds of all reason. True, this daring impious wretch has "rushed in where angels fear to tread," and blasphemously impugned the good sense and the judgment of the civil service! Heaven help him, what blasphemy!—that is what has roused your ire so!'

'But Mastodon knows nothing of this: he, too, is not influenced by such petty motives, which, upon my soul, Murray, you ought to have known better than attribute to me. Mastodon is a first-rate fellow, though he is one of the "service" you, too, seem to hate so much; Mastodon cannot be influenced by these considerations. He has seen inflammatory treasonable documents with this man's name attached to them, calling on the natives to rise and massacre us; and when I talk of calling him to account for this, you say I am actuated by motives of revenge because he has abused the service!—my service!'

'Well, Dacres, calm yourself; for heaven's sake, don't act on this despatch of Mastodon's: you yourself have told me often, that you have received proofs of innumerable plots and conspiracies that have been going on all around us, involving us in their interminable folds like a huge spider's web. All sorts of juggling and imposture and forgery, and counterfeit characters and writing, are employed; no devilry, no artifice that can be made use of to deceive and entangle us, and insure our ultimate ruin, has been passed over;—you admit all this, and you admit it is all going on now: why, then, may not this be a part of the same machinery? why may not this letter of Mastodon's—you can't recognise his handwriting—why may not this letter be a trick intended to sow the seeds of discord in our little camp? Depend on it, you had better leave the matter alone: it will all come right in the end, and explain itself,—that is, if we get out of this hobble, as I said before; and, if not, God knows, it does not much matter: Thurston, if he is a traitor, can't do us much harm.'

'Has he been talking to you again about Asgar Ally?'

'Why, really, I am almost afraid to tell you, Dacres, lest you should order a drumhead court-martial on him, and hang him. But, to tell the truth, he has been most pertinaciously obstinate in endeavouring to persuade me Asgar Ally is a traitor; and, strange to say, though he is so fond of blowing the trumpet for natives, and makes out that they are ten times better than Englishmen, he wanted me to persuade you and others to shoot or hang Asgar Ally—on the plea that he "was only a native."'

'Only a native! well, that is good: and this from the philanthropic M.P.! And pray what do you infer from this?'

'Why, nothing further than that he is persuaded, as also *were* several members of our garrison for a long time, and some may be so still, that Asgar Ally is deceiving us, and that our only safety consists in putting him beyond the reach of doing us any injury.'

'Good God! what fearful ingratitude!—as if Asgar Ally, even if he was what you——'

'Not I.'

'I beg your pardon—what Thurston says,

a traitor; even if he was, what harm could he do us that would justify such a course of action?'

'No, I do not say it could be justified. I agree with you in trusting Asgar Ally fully, implicitly. I think the services he has done us have been incalculable—absolutely incalculable. I doubt if we should have been alive now if it had not been for him; I consider we owe him our lives; and if we survive this, I hope to see him amply rewarded. No reward could be too much. But all this is nothing to the point. Thurston is persuaded he is a traitor—he is honestly persuaded of it—and thinks our only safety consists in putting him where he can't do us any harm.'

'But how can he do us any harm, even if he wished?'

'Why, he could insure our ruin by showing the secret communication into the tomb. Do you not see how much depends on this? It is morally certain that they will attack this place with heavy artillery: nay, perhaps to-morrow they will open a fire against the house which it cannot withstand an hour—they are certain to do this sooner or later; it must come to our all making for the tomb. We may there elude their grasp for a little while; and just now every hour gained increases our chance of final escape a hundred-fold. Reinforcements are sure to come here from Aurungabad or Mitterpore, or both; it all depends upon whether we can hold out for a day or so whether, when they come, they will find us alive or dead. If our plan succeeds, and the ladies when the artillery opens fire make good their retreat into that passage, and the house is thrown down afterwards—a mass of ruins, which we must take care it is,—access on this side is cut off: on the other we are far stronger even than we are here, for the Nawab's guns will not make a breach in the old tomb very easily. On the other hand, if we are betrayed, and attacked from this side and from that at once, we shall be caught like rabbits in a warren, a dog at one end and a ferret at the other. This is Thurston's argument, and there is much in it that is very sound. He says, Asgar Ally will betray us.'

'He forgets that the existence of the passage is known to at least one individual in the enemy's camp.'

'He does not believe that it is.'

'How does he know?'

'Nay, this you must ask him, not me; he says his information is good.'

'His information! and his experience, too! I'll tell you what, Murray, I believe he is just such another as that incarnate fiend they have yonder hounding on these wild beasts to get our blood; and, what's more, I believe Asgar Ally knows something about the villain.'

'Have you ever asked him?'

'No; but I will, the first time I see him.—Ha! who is this? here he is, by Jove, just the very person!'

It was indeed Asgar Ally himself. He was coming from the direction of the enemy's camp, and met the two officers just at the entrance of the fortification between the two redoubts where they had been holding the conversation related above. It was very dark, and consequently Asgar Ally was not perceived till he had come up quite close to them.

'Where are you come from, Asgar Ally?' asked Dacres.

'I have been almost down to the kaffirs' camp, sahib,' he replied. 'It is so dark, and their sentries keep so bad a look-out, that I got down quite close to their lines, and crept along the ground on my belly up to the outside of their advance battery. They are getting heavy guns up, sahib, and they will open fire to-night or to-morrow morning.'

'They cannot see to open fire to-night,' said Murray; 'it is too dark.'

'No. We must be very careful to show no

lights. Did you see anything else, Asgar Ally? any preparation for an assault?'

'No, sahib. They will not assault again till they have fired the big guns for a day or two.'

'Tell me, Asgar Ally, do you know this sahib at all?'

'What sahib?'

'That sahib that escaped with you from the mutineers' camp, that they were going to burn, you said—do you know who he is?'

'Ah, sahib, why should I talk about such things? The men do say foolish things about him; but I tell them they know nothing, and they don't understand the customs of the English sahib.'

'What have you heard about him?'

'I do not like to say—it is not fit to repeat.'

'Tell me—it shall do you no harm—no one shall hear it but Captain Murray and myself—come, tell us, what is it?'

Asgar Ally might have been about to speak and to disclose something wonderful, perhaps, but they were interrupted by Murray, who suddenly called out—

'Who goes there?'

'It is I,' a voice answered from the gloom, but so close that it was a wonder they had not seen the speaker before: he was standing within three paces of Murray, and hidden, till he moved out of the shade of it, behind an angle of the parapet of the redoubt.

'Who? Ha, Thurston! talk of the devil, you know—' Dacres whispered to Murray: 'he has been listening, and must have heard every word. Where are you come from?' continued Dacres, addressing the new arrival, and speaking rather sharply.

'From the rear of the fortification—I have been going my rounds; there are people prowling about that have no business to be.'

'There are, indeed,' said Dacres, significantly.

'Look!' cried Murray and Asgar Ally together, as if the attention of the whole party had not been simultaneously arrested.

In an instant, from the rear of the house there arose a bright blue light, that brought the whole outline of the house and the neighbouring defences in bold relief against the dark sky.

'Treachery!' shouted Dacres, 'd——d treachery! Some one has lit blue lights, to show our position: now look out—they will open fire.'

It was as he said; blue lights had been used to show the position: they remained burning full a minute, during which time the enemy had pointed their guns, or tried to do so, for, as the lights were suddenly extinguished, probably from some member of the garrison on duty on the rear post having rushed down and put them out, the batteries opened fire, and one, two, three, four balls came swishing through the air, just after the flash and the report had warned the anxious spectators what to look for. At the second discharge, one of the enemy's guns burst with a tremendous explosion; but they kept up the fire with the other three.

Dacres, Murray, and Thurston separated to repair to their respective posts. In the hurry of the moment, Dacres forgot to say anything more to Asgar Ally; in fact, he lost sight of him in the dark. The garrison remained under arms all night. The fire from the enemy's batteries, though irritating, did no injury, as they had failed to get the range, or lay their guns properly. The ladies and children, meantime, made the best of their way into the secret passage, and spent the night in conveying their bedding and other little necessaries into the tomb, for the destruction of their present defences was now inevitable.

The sky was cloudy, and it was very dark all night; all looked anxiously forward to the dawn, for it seemed likely enough that the coming day would seal the fate of many. It was hardly to be doubted that the enemy would attack in force. Dacres, who was everywhere, looking now after the movement of the non-combatants, and now rushing up to the redoubt to speak a word of encouragement or to see all right, and now at his own post in the rear, was coming out of the house just after the first streak of daylight appeared in the eastern horizon, for he wanted to give some parting injunction to Murray in the front redoubt before the active operations, in which there was little doubt they would soon have their hands full, commenced. As he entered the garden, he suddenly confronted Thurston, who was coming in, and, not seeing him, ran against him. He stammered out an apology and passed on. He had not gone ten paces, before, stretched on the garden path, with the blood flowing from a recently-inflicted wound in the forehead, his features stiff in death, lay the corpse of Asgar Ally. Dacres was absolutely struck dumb with horror. There could not be a doubt of it, this was Thurston's handiwork,—the noble, the faithful, devoted Asgar Ally slain by the hand of a murderer. Murray had just distinguished Dacres's form in the twilight of the morning, and came out of the redoubt to meet him. He, too, stood petrified with horror. They looked from the body of the murdered man enquiringly into each other's face ; at last Dacres spoke.

'Now do you believe me, Murray? it was he that did it.'

'I heard a pistol-shot but a minute ago,' said Murray.

'And I met Thurston as I came out; he was going in—straight from this direction!'

'Look! here he comes!'

Dacres turned as Thurston came up; he fixed his eyes sternly on him.

'Thurston, is this your work?' he said.

'It is. I have taken the law into my own hands, and saved your lives,—that is, saved them if they are to be saved at all; if not, it was no crime to deprive this man of what he would have lost anyhow in an hour or two. This is no time to stick at trifles, or wrangle about words.'

'Indeed it isn't; but as sure as there's a God in heaven, you shall answer for this!'

'So be it, Mr. Dacres. I will answer for it when and where you choose, so you have authority to demand an explanation from me. I have only acted as any right-minded Englishman would have acted under the circumstances. Besides, why this fuss? 'tis only a native after all.'

Any rejoinder to this remark from the philanthropist, so illustrative of the variance we at times discover between theory and practice, was cut short by a tremendous fire of musketry and cannonade that was opened from the enemy's batteries, and from a large force of infantry they had pushed up during the night to within a short distance of the fortification. The attack soon became general.

CHAPTER LII.

Heavy as was the fire the defenders were exposed to, and threatening the attitude assumed by the enemy, it soon became apparent that the latter had no real intention of coming to close quarters till they had wearied out the besieged, and battered down their defences by a long and protracted use of their artillery. The consequence was, that the efforts of Dacres and his gallant little band were necessarily confined to acting on the defensive, to watching the effect of the cannonade, wondering how long it would be before their defences were destroyed, and wishing for the night. The ladies had all long ago left the house, as I have said, and were safe from present danger in the tomb, to which they had now removed all their little stock of furniture and belongings. The garrison, finding there was no chance of the enemy coming within range even of their one gun, much less their smaller firearms, evacuated the redoubt and outer defences during the heat of the day, and took refuge from the rays of the sun under cover of the house, where, however, they were obliged to be constantly on the look-out, for every now and then a ball struck some more frangible part of the walls and brought down a quantity of stones and plaster. The ladies, with the assistance of the few, very few servants that had remained faithful to them, prepared their food in the tomb, and brought it up to their gallant defenders.

Towards the afternoon, however, parties were seen leaving the enemy's battery and advancing towards the fortification. It seemed too strong a body for reconnoitring only, and not strong enough for an attack. Dacres therefore feared some stratagem, and was against taking any steps to oppose them. Murray, however, who had the command, and who was cheerfully obeyed by all, took a different view, and resolved to attack if they came sufficiently close to render it feasible. They accordingly watched the cautious approach of this party with considerable interest, and finding that they were coming closer and closer, Murray determined to attack them. He led the sortie himself, well followed up by a chosen party of a dozen of the officers and nearly all the natives: among the former Thurston was conspicuous for energy and daring. The sortie was eminently successful: they came up to within a hundred paces of the enemy unobserved, when firing a volley, they charged with the bayonet. The ground just in this spot was covered with shrubs and bushes, which afforded excellent cover to an advancing party. The enemy, brought up with the sudden discharge of musketry and rifles, which made a number of gaps in their ranks, were panic-struck, and being uncertain of the strength of the body opposed to them, no sooner had the latter made their appearance, rushing upon their foe with dauntless courage, and shouting as they charged, than they took to their heels. Murray would not follow them up, determined not to be drawn into an ambuscade, but contented himself with halting his band and firing at the retreating enemy as long as they were within range. After this, they returned to the fortification to receive the congratulation of their comrades. Except this, nothing occurred during the day to vary the monotony—if monotony it can be called—of remaining on the defensive watching the active though distant efforts of an enemy to insure your destruction.

Just as the evening drew on, Murray suggested to Dacres the daring scheme of making a sortie right into the enemy's battery, and, if possible, spiking their guns. The credit of the first suggestion of the scheme, he said, was due to Thurston, who had first proposed it to him and demonstrated its practicability. The contempt, it seems, he had now conceived for native valour, was only equal to the admiration he had before expressed of the many virtues of the native character. It was a bold and daring plan, but if successful, the advantage gained would be enormous. Delay was everything, and it was worth a great risk attempting it.

After the fate of Asgar Ally, Dacres resolutely determined not to hold any further communication with the man he now regarded as a murderer. Indeed, he had resolved, if their lives were spared and they were rescued from their present peril, to bring him to account for this atrocious crime, if he was not dealt with to the utmost rigour of the law for the other and grave offence of which he stood charged—nay, in Dacres's own mind convicted—by the accusation of Sir Marmaduke. It would have been, however, most injudicious to have interfered with him under present circumstances, where he was not only very useful, and where every additional arm and head was worth just now their weight in gold twice counted, but since his late exhibition of true courage and manly daring in the sortie he had become one of the most popular characters in the garrison. The murder of Asgar Ally, favourite as he had been, was deeply felt by many of them, but they had little time to think or to enquire into the story, and most of them took for granted that Thurston, true Englishman as he was now at the eleventh hour showing himself to be, must have had some very good reason for acting as he had; others did not scruple to say that they no longer trusted any native to such an extent as to suppose that any one of them, even of those outwardly most staunch and faithful, might not at any given moment lay himself open to a charge of treachery, and deserve to be dealt with summarily, even as Thurston had dealt with Asgar Ally; while in truth all of them had become so hardened to suffering, so inured to scenes of death, so reckless of human life, owing to the continued hardships and dangers they had passed through, that they had ceased to regard the act of depriving a fellow-creature of life, even in cold blood, at all in the light we are accustomed to view such deeds.

When men or women have the prospect of death steadily before their eyes for a long time, they grow callous to the sight of suffering to an extent they would have thought utterly impossible till the actual experiment had been made. Nature seems to provide a remedy for herself in some cases. It seems mercifully ordained that wounds which would under ordinary circumstances ruin the intellect and unseat the reason, are cauterised the moment they are inflicted. Extreme hardships and sufferings have a hardening effect on the mind; they gradually deaden our sensibilities, and prevent us from feeling very acutely the stroke of calamity when it comes upon us, after we have passed through an apprenticeship of sorrow. We often read of people undergoing trials and enduring mental agonies which we fancy sufficient to destroy life or produce insanity—but the effect may not actually be felt with anything like the intensity we imagine, owing to the process the mind may have gone through previously, not only purified, but naturally hardened to a degree of insensibility in the furnace of affliction. And it is a source of no little relief to those whose dearly-loved relatives or friends may have been exposed to the terrible fate that overtook so many of our fellow-countrymen in 1857. To them, when death did come, it must have come shorn of more than half its terrors. I speak not of the hope that faith whispered in the souls of so many, pointing with wonderful vividness, as the end drew near, to a rest and deliverance beyond the valley of the shadow of death, but of the effect of mere outward circumstances upon the feelings and the moral sense.

But I am digressing. From these and other causes, the murder of Asgar Ally—for murder it most unquestionably was—created about as much excitement among the little garrison, as in ordinary times would have been awakened by the wanton slaughter of a pet animal,—hardly as much, perhaps. It was not because Asgar Ally was a native, though the philanthropist did allege that in justification, but merely that they had grown callous to the loss of human life, and did not, in short, think it worth making a fuss about.

The antipathy which Dacres felt towards Thurston, and the deeply-settled conviction that the latter was what Sir Marmaduke evidently believed him to be, would not allow him, as I said, to hold any communication with him. He, however, talked over the suggestion of a desperate sortie under cover of the night with Murray, and, having at length agreed on the proposed plan, nothing remained but for them to carry it out. The greatest danger to be apprehended, was lest the enemy should make an attack on their position while a large part of the garrison were absent. To obviate this, it would be necessary to leave a good strong guard behind: and how was that to be done, providing at the same time a sufficiently strong party for the attack? It was at length decided that Dacres, with Burleigh and two others, should remain behind with all the sepoys, except those that should volunteer: the whole of the remainder of the garrison were to form the sortie.

As soon as night set in, and it became dark enough for men to move about without much danger of being seen, the attacking party crept quietly and cautiously down to the outside of the batteries without attracting the notice of a single sentry. Sentries, in fact, there were none; for nothing was further from the imagination of the rebels, than that the poor doomed band of 'kaffirs,' whom they looked upon as wild beasts caught in a trap, should venture on so bold a display. The consequence was, that our friends had actually clambered up through the embrasure and were in the battery before they were observed. The alarm, however, was then soon given: such confusion and tumult followed,—such yelling and shouting—such random, reckless firing—such running hither and thither of officers and men—such neighing of horses, and trumpeting of frightened elephants—such an uproar and clash of mingled swords, that one might have imagined the inhabitants of Pandemonium had all been turned loose upon the spot. Murray and his party kept well together; this was the prearranged plan. They cut down the guard at the first gun, spiked it, blew up the ammunition-waggons, and then went on to the next as steadily and methodically as if they were going through the rehearsal of a play. It may be imagined, however, that they did not lose any time unnecessarily; there was every prospect of their having rather hot work, and much remained to be accomplished. The second gun they managed as easily as the first: the guard, now completly panic-struck, fled without opposing them. At the third they were met by a large body of the enemy, who had collected just at the foot of the battery, and rushed in a body on the sortie. Murray was in the act of hammering the spike into the vent; Thurston stood immediately behind him; the rest were all round hotly engaged, for the attack was general. Two of the enemy forced themselves through the *mêlée*, and reaching Murray, struck at him simultaneously. Thurston's eye, however, was on them; with his revolver he shot one through the heart, and with his sword warded off the blow that would but for this have cleft Murray's head in two. The next instant, the assailant lay dead, wounded in half-a-dozen different places.

The struggle now became most desperate. The Englishmen were opposed by a force fifty times their number; but the magnitude of the odds against them made in reality but little difference; in fact, it operated in their favour. For though their assailants were a hundred to one, in the confined space in which the conflict was raging, but a very few could get to the front or take any actual share in the work: the consequence was, that the enemy's superiority in numbers went for nothing, or next to it. The bulk of them were afraid to fire; for, being in the rear, the chances were they shot down their own friends, and those in front could not do more than contend singly with their antagonists, for whom they were in actual hand-to-hand conflict no match at all. It was something the same state of things as that described by Macaulay.

> Was none who would be foremost,
>   To lead such dire attack;
> But those behind cried 'Forward,'
>   And those before cried 'Back:'
> And backward now and forward,
>   Waver the deep array.

How many times in the history of India

and of Asia has it been proved that numbers beyond a certain limit are in reality no additional element of strength! You read of mighty conquerors assembling armies of hundreds of thousands to oppose a much smaller force: of what use are the majority of these hundreds of thousands? In proportion to the smallness of the force to be opposed, the number actually engaged must be small too: the rest may shout, and raise a tumult and urge on, if they can, their comrades in the front; but, as a general rule, they only create confusion, and do a great deal more harm than good.

Murray and his comrades steadily kept their end in view, to spike all the guns in the battery before they left. There had been six: one had burst, and they managed to spike four; the other it was beyond their power to get at—they could not even approach it, so dense was the crowd of rebel sepoys by which it was surrounded.

'We must give it up!' cried Murray. 'Are you all ready? Follow me into the ditch; then clear out and make the best of our way back. Now!'

And away they went, leaping over the earthen parapet and alighting safely in the ditch: but they had a desperate struggle, for many of the rebels had gone round with a view to intercepting their retreat. They cut their way through, however, and, favoured by the darkness of the night, made good their retreat. When the survivors reached the fortified house, exhausted, all more or less severely wounded, covered with dirt and black with gunpowder, they counted heads: out of thirteen who had gone on that desperate enterprise, but eight returned. Among those who had fallen, whose names had been prominently mentioned in this narrative, were Barncliffe and Hornby: two sepoys had accompanied them, and they too had not returned.

The success, however, was most complete and satisfactory; they had gained a respite, and of what value might it not be! There was no danger of the garrison being disturbed that night; but Dacres and the others who had remained behind insisted on taking all the responsibility of watch and ward upon themselves, and leaving the others to seek undisturbed the rest they so much needed.

'You will shake hands with him now, will you not?' said Murray, addressing Dacres, and pointing to Thurston, who had already stretched himself on the bare ground in an attitude betokening complete prostration. 'He has behaved splendidly: he saved my life; and, indeed, for the whole plan was his, he has probably, in one sense, saved all our lives.' He said this just before he left the post to visit his wife, and report to her and the other ladies the result of the night's operations. For some of them he would have but bad news.

'No, don't ask me,' said Dacres. 'I cannot shake hands with him, stained as they are with the blood of the innocent, even as the guilt of infinitely greater crimes has stained his soul. However, dog as he is, as long as he fights and uses his teeth in the proper way I won't interfere with him; but shake hands—never!'

The following day was one of cessation of active hostilities. The enemy were busily engaged, as Dacres could easily see through his glass, in remedying the damage done to their guns. They made no attack, however, the whole day, but on the following morning they had succeeded in drilling out the spikes from three of the guns, or else they had mounted others, for they opened fire at dawn from four pieces of ordnance. Still the result of the successful sortie could not yet be told: it had gained them certainly a clear twenty-four hours. Again and again did that postscript to Sir Marmaduke's letter occur to Dacres's mind. 'I leave this to-morrow for Aurungabad, and I may come your way.' He counted the days, and calculated over and over again how long it would take Sir Marmaduke to ride across country to Aurungabad, and how long it would take Harley—for Graham, he felt convinced, was dead—to get there. Should they happily meet, there was no doubt that their rescue would be attempted by Sir Marmaduke himself; and he had every confidence in his activity and judgment, and knew he could rely on his sympathy. If it could be effected by anybody, it would be by him. Then he thought what a mere chance, a mere probability he was building on as a secure foundation—that Sir Marmaduke and Harley should accidentally meet at Aurungabad. It was not likely the latter would remain there an hour longer than was necessary; and why should fortune, that had played them so many cruel tricks of late, be benign this once and bring Mastodon and Harley together? Not once only, or twenty times, did these reflections pass and repass through Dacres's mind; and they always ended with the thought, 'Well, thank God! we gained twenty-four hours at least.'

To batter down a house built of brick masonry, however, with heavy artillery, is after all but an easy task. It was painfully evident that the time was rapidly approaching when it would be necessary to evacuate the old ruined tenement, and take to their last stronghold—as, in one sense, it is destined to be the last resting-place of us all—the tomb.

Tombs are put to queer purposes sometimes in the East—not such tombs—

> With many a rhyme and uncouth sculpture decked—

as the 'rustic moralist learning to die' wanders among in a country churchyard in our native land—but huge massive dome-shaped buildings large enough to quarter a regiment in. Many of these domed tombs have been turned into dwelling-houses, and excellent dwelling-houses they make. The walls are of such enormous thickness that they keep out the heat far more effectually than the thickest thatch or most excellently-contrived roof the would-be luxurious Englishman puts between his head and the sun. Incongruous as it may seem to English notions, many is the time I have witnessed gay scenes and sumptuous feasts and listened to the strains of music to which pretty feet were keeping time, as the dancers tripped along in the polka or the waltz, or enjoyed the romp of a Sir Roger de Coverley, in these buildings sacred to the memory of defunct ladies and gentlemen of the past age:

to such vile uses do we sometimes put our—no, other people's—tombs in the East!

On the afternoon of the second day after the rebels had recommenced their artillery practice, Dacres and Murray came to the conclusion that it was necessary to abandon the house. The walls had been so battered that it was impossible they could withstand another hour's cannonade. A general muster was accordingly taken, and all hands assembled. They had to clear away a good deal of rubbish and débris which had fallen, even since they began seriously to contemplate the necessity of removing, before they could open up a way to their retreat. It was done, however, and they gained in safety the little room which communicated with the entrance to the subterranean passage. Everything had been removed beforehand, and the whole party went down, except Dacres and Murray, who remained watching for the final catastrophe. And it came. The lower part of the walls no longer served as a support to the upper; every shot told upon its battered weakened state with tremendous effect. By twos and threes, and then in handsful, the bricks fell out. As each ball struck, each time the building shook like an aspen leaf. The climax was not long in coming; there was a crash like the roar of a waterfall or a continuous clap of thunder, and down it came. Murray and Dacres saved themselves in time, and when they reached their friends in the tomb, the entrance to their retreat from one side was protected most satisfactorily by a mass of ruins which would take the enemy, unaided, a week to clear away.

CHAPTER LIII.

GREAT was the exultation of the rebels when they saw the house fall into ruins, for they took for granted that now the hated kaffirs must be either smashed to atoms, or, if there were any survivors to be dug out alive from the débris, they would necessarily become an easy capture. And their consternation and astonishment were proportionally great when they found, on searching the ruins, which they could now do unmolested, that there were no traces whatever of the expected prey. The Mirza, who it is more than probable might have aided in the solution of this mystery, was either absent or engaged in affairs of his own, or for some reason did not choose to offer the explanation which he most undoubtedly could have given had he liked.

Dacres and Murray, after consultation with the other officers, had resolved upon keeping their present position a secret as long as possible, but not to allow this secrecy to interfere with the resistance and defence to which they must ultimately attribute their delivery, if delivery, indeed, was to come at all.

It was not until the afternoon of the next day that it became known to the rebels where their enemies were ensconced, at least it was not till then that the former commenced active operations for an attack upon the new position. This was begun in the usual manner by the erection of batteries, and placing the heavy guns in position out of reach of the musketry fire from the defenders. This done, they opened fire as before, and kept it up pretty well, except at intervals, all night. The massive walls, however, of the old Saiyad's tomb afforded far greater resistance than the comparatively slender defence of the more modern-built dwelling-house, and the cannonade appeared at first to produce little or no effect. Great danger, indeed, was experienced from the balls when they ricocheted into the inside of the tomb, the splinters and fragments of stone flying about in all directions, and inflicting awkward wounds.

Very considerable protection, however, was afforded by the redoubt which had been erected opposite the entrance to the tomb, whose thick earthen embankments generally allowed the cannon shot to sink into them harmlessly. The enemy were evidently afraid to come to close quarters, and seemed determined to try either to weary out or to starve the garrison into submission.

That had diminished much in numbers since the outbreak of the rebellion. Poor Mrs. Barncliffe never survived the blow of her husband's death: she breathed her last the second night after they moved into the tomb, the same that saw the death of her husband. Her sufferings at the last were acute, but short: she died in giving birth to a child, whose soul had already been mercifully taken by its Creator, before it was ushered into a world of suffering and sorrow.

The ladies that now remained were Mrs. Murray, Mrs. Wetherall, Miss Trinchinopoly, and Amy Leslie, of those who have before been presented to my readers. There were, besides, Mrs. Schleiermacher, the wife of the missionary, whose individual share in the adventures and sufferings recounted in this narrative have not been noticed merely to avoid swelling the number of the dramatis personæ to an inconvenient extent. Mrs. Schleiermacher had four children, all of whom with herself survived, till the present crisis, the horrors of the mutiny. There were, besides, Mrs. Jamieson and three children, the family of Sergeant Jamieson of the commissariat department. And that was all that remained of the gentle sex and of the children among the garrison. Most of them had borne up bravely against the tremendous brunt of woe that had come thus suddenly upon them—Mrs. Murray particularly. The mutiny and the hardships she had to undergo, the anxiety she was doomed to suffer, seemed to have had the effect of totally changing her character. Whereas before the outbreak she had been, as far as intellectual attainments go, a commonplace person, she had now become quite the contrary. Before she was one of those women that seem formed for ornament alone and not for use—and indeed such a beautiful creature was well able to fulfill the part nature apparently designed her for; but now she was all energy and self-devotion, thinking little of herself and much of others; she was always ready and on the look-out for opportunity to do some unselfish action. Regardless of danger or of toil, she would take part with her husband in the sterner duties that devolved upon him, and this without losing one iota of that delicacy and refinement and feminine grace that give to the gentler sex the greatest and most valued of their charms.

Amy was heart-broken; but her spirits somehow kept up. The future of this life had no very cheering prospects for her; all was blank, even when she could bring herself to look with anything like hope beyond the gloomy mist of danger and death that now encircled their horizon. She was still capable of doing much, and in activity she found the greatest relief from the burden of her sorrows. Mrs. Schleiermacher was, I am sorry to say, shiftless and useless; she could scarcely be made to understand the necessity of looking after her own children—she did not even attempt this as long as there was anyone else to relieve her of the duty. Her good husband, about whom I should have liked to have said more had time and space permitted me, fought and prayed, and prayed and fought alternately, in a fashion that brought to the recollection of those who witnessed his valour mingled with devotion, and devotion mingled with valour, the character of the old covenanters described by Walter Scott. Mrs. Wetherall, like others in her condition, had become marvellously soon reconciled to the loss of her affectionate husband. It was from no want of real depth of feeling—no lack of true affection—no affectation, much less reality, of heartlessness—but simply and solely the effects which the presence of constant danger and hardship, with death in all its forms perpetually before the eyes, produces in the character whether of men or women. Miss Trinchinopoly afforded an instance of the way in which the delicate flower of love can bloom and blossom even under the most adverse circumstances, and in the most rocky soil. Yet in these adverse circumstances—amid these dreadful scenes, with death staring them in the face and cannon within a short distance of them firing day and night—even here did the tender passion strike its roots deeper and deeper into the soil and twine its tendrils round the heart of Dr. Mactartan. In his own rough way, and with the little leisure for wooing that any of them enjoyed, he had nevertheless wooed and won the heart of Maria Trinchinopoly, and she was his betrothed for earth—if they got safe out of their tomb—if not, for heaven.

Strange is it to see what creatures of habit we are. Here in the terrible circumstances I have attempted to detail, with thousands of savage fanatics yelling for their blood all around them—with cannon shot battering their defences, beneath which they crouched for protection, and occasionally finding a way even into their little circle—did this family, for such they were, carry on their daily duties, indulge in fancies and hopes of the future, talk over the past, and speculate on their probable deliverance, just as if that deliverance was at hand. They found time to make love and to quarrel, to talk a little innocent scandal, nay, occasionally to indulge in a joke. They ate and drank and slept (those who were not actively engaged); the ladies attended to their avocations, nursed the children, gave them food, heard the elder ones say their prayers night and morning, put them to bed, dressed and washed them (though sparing in their ablutions, for water was scarce and precious) in the morning, as if they were in their own houses pursuing their ordinary course of domestic life.

Upon the character of none of the garrison had so great a change been wrought by the events they had passed through as upon Thurston. All his philanthropic feelings had evaporated and given place to impulse of such a contrary tendency, that Dacres, who actually hated the man, could not help thinking sometimes that he was doing him an injustice, and that he could not be held accountable for his actions. The officers, however, who did not share the commissioner's dislike, were rather amused at watching the change that had come over his spirit. In his hostility to natives and hatred of them he was now the foremost; his thirst for their blood seemed really insatiable. For hours he would sit in the burning sun, rifle in hand, resting on his knee, watching through his loophole, in the hope of getting a shot. Whenever he was lucky enough to get one he became almost frantic. 'Another of the cursed brutes,' he would cry, clapping his hands and looking round with glee; or as he leant forward to take aim he might be heard muttering, 'Now for one of the black devils.' He never spoke of them as anything but 'black devils;' and even the faithful and gallant little band of sepoys, who had in spite of such tremendous temptation remained staunch, were afraid to go near the 'poggle sahib' (the mad sahib), as they called him, for if they did, or if they addressed him, he would turn upon them with the most dreadful oaths and the foulest abuse. It might be supposed that all this would have gone some way to prove to Dacres that he was wrong in the view he took of Thurston's character; but, on the contrary, it only confirmed him in his suspicions.

'The fellow is acting,' he used to say—'only acting; all this is only a disguise assumed to hoodwink and deceive us—if he is not mad.'

Through evil report and good report, however, did Thurston pursue the tenor of his way, killing as many natives as he could; where he could not kill, wounding; when he could do neither, cursing. They say adversity shows a man's character, and displays his true colours. If so, it did not bring out that of Mr. Thurston's in a very enviable light, for he exhibited all the symptoms of a cowardly selfish spirit, vilifying his own fellow-countrymen when he could make political capital by it, and when threatened with pains and penalties on his own carcase, behaving with the ferocity of a tiger or a wolf.

I must, however, leave the brave garrison to describe what befell Leila during the few eventful days that had just clapsed.

She gained early intimation that her husband had been forcibly taken from his palace, and if she were in any doubt as to the truth of the reports that were brought, they were speedily set at rest by her finding herself a prisoner. She had intimated to her attendants her intention of accompanying her husband, or rather following him, into captivity, but soon found that her authority had passed away. The women-servants told her, with a disrespectful grin, that they had orders to see that she did not leave the palace. When asked 'Who gave those orders?' they refused to tell, but Leila had no difficulty in guessing.

She was then compelled to remain in her own apartment, where she ruminated on the fickleness of fortune, and the baseness or ingratitude of mankind. So passed the first day of her captivity.

In the evening she was disturbed by the entrance of the most ungainly, unprepossessing person she had ever seen. This was a tall, gaunt, grey-haired, shrivelled-up old woman, over whom trouble rather than time had drawn its blighting withering touch. But her eyes retained all the fire and spirit of youth, without either its tenderness of expression or guilelessness. The old hag, without asking permission to enter, or going through any of the forms of ceremonial respect that Leila had been accustomed to from everyone that approached her, came in and seated herself in the corner of the room, keeping her little black eyes fixed on the mistress of the apartment, and grinning all the time.

'Who are you, and what do you want here?' said Leila, drying her tears, and assuming for a moment her wonted dignity of manner and address.

The old hag seemed deaf or dumb, or both, for she only shook her head from side to side, grinning all the time.

'Who are you?' repeated Leila. 'I insist

on your telling me, or leaving this apartment at once. What business have you here, and who sent you?'

Still no answer.

Leila arose and went towards the door, with a view of endeavouring to obtain assistance. As she approached the corner of the room where the old hag was seated, the latter stretched out a long bony arm and caught her dress. Leila shrank back from the touch as if it polluted her, gathered up the folds of her dress in her hand, and retreated a pace or two, looking all the time steadily at the old woman in the corner, as if she was some loathsome reptile. Then, for the first time, the old creature opened her mouth and said—

'Stay, lady; you need not be afraid, I shall not hurt you; only, if you make a disturbance, it will be unpleasant for you. Stay quiet and no one shall hurt you. I have my orders to watch you day and night—watch you, that is all. I will not touch you, as you don't like it, though you need not shrink from me as if I polluted you. I was once as young and beautiful as you—not so very long ago either—and it will not be so very long, I dare say, before you are as old and ugly-looking as I—he! he! he!'

There was something horribly malicious in

the chuckling croak of the old wretch. Leila absolutely loathed her. She said nothing, however, and the old woman went on.

'Yes, lady, my orders are never to take my eyes off you, whether you eat or sleep, or whatever you do, or wherever you go—though you cannot go very far just now—he! he! he! I am a very light sleeper, and the least movement awakes me, so it will not matter if I do go to sleep.'

'Orders! who gave you orders? Who sent you here, I ask you? Tell me at once, or I will summon my women, and have you whipped out of the palace.'

The old hag went off into such a fit of chuckling at this threat that Leila thought she would have choked herself in the fit of coughing that followed.

'Orders!' she said, as soon as she had recovered herself sufficiently to speak intelligibly. 'By his order who is master here now; by his order that men and devils obey. He will come soon and explain it all himself; meantime I watch you, night and day, eating and sleeping, walking and sitting—night and day—night and day!'

Leila shrank instinctively from asking more particulars: she became really alarmed, and changed her tone.

'Listen, my good woman,' she said. 'I have gold and jewels enough to make you rich—richer than ever you dreamed of being. I will give them all—all—if you will help me to escape from this place. Help me to get away to my husband.'

'There, now you speak like a sweet lady, as you are. We had better be friends, I promise you. Let me see some of these precious jewels of yours, my lady-bird; I like jewels. Are they fine ones?'

'Oh, yes, magnificent ones! I will show them to you.' And going to a casket in another corner of the room she unlocked it, and displayed to the old hag two splendid necklaces of pearls and emeralds.

'Let me look, let me look,' said the old hag, stretching out her long arms, and speaking with all the earnestness a covetous thirst for the precious baubles awakened in her miserly heart. 'Let me look. Ah, they are fine—fine indeed! And how much is this one worth?' she added, holding up to the light the necklace Leila had meantime given her.

'That one is worth ten thousand rupees,' she said, pointing to the pearl one—'so my husband said when he gave it me; and the other is yet more valuable still. Both are yours, my good woman. Keep them, and help a poor unfortunate lady in her distress.'

'The blessings of Alla on your sweet pretty head!' she said; 'you are as liberal as Hatim Tai. Yes, I will keep them, and never forget you, be sure,' she added, putting them away in her bosom; 'but I dare not disobey orders—you don't know my master yet—yet, he! he! he!—or you would not counsel me to disobey him. I did once, but never will again. Look here, this is what I got for being so rash.'

So saying she turned her back towards the lady, and, taking off the loose muslin robe that encircled her wasted withered form, disclosed to the astonished and disgusted Leila her bare back, scarred all over with marks of scourging.

Leila shrunk back more horrified than ever: still she was touched with a feeling of sorrow at the marks of suffering and brutal treatment undergone by one of her own sex, ungainly though she was.

'Who did that?'

'He—he did it. Ah lady! my story is a sad one, but I am not the only one that has suffered. I was once young and beautiful like you, when he took me, and I lived like a princess for some years, till I grew ugly and my hair turned grey—for I loved him then, ah! I loved him as you, lady, loved your husband—but he was false to me—he grew tired of me and took to other women, and made me a slave in the palace where I had been a mistress before, and a slave I am now. I shall be your slave, lady, when you go to live with him.'

'I go—I live with him—I!—you are mad, you old wretch, to talk to me like this. I would die—I will kill myself before his hated polluted hand shall touch me. If evil has befallen my poor husband—he who was so good, so noble, so generous—Alla will protect me—Alla will take my life sooner than I shall be delivered to such a son of Satan as he.'

'Do not talk of killing yourself, lady; it is to prevent that that I am sent to watch you.'

'You prevent me—you watch me! but come, I have given you jewels enough to purchase your freedom and make you comfortable for the rest of your life. Aid me to escape and I will double them.'

'Listen, lady—I dare not: his power is so great, he can see what we are doing and hear what we are saying, though he is far away. Do not talk of escape—be patient and wait. He is gone to the wars; perhaps Alla may befriend us yet, and a bullet from the hand of the kaffirs may take away his accursed life; but now, as long as he lives, there is no help for it: we are in his power, and we must obey him.'

'You will not let me go? you will not help me?'

'Alas, lady, I cannot if I would! All your servants and attendants have been changed, except those who are in his pay; the outer gates are locked, and every door and window is watched from the outside day and night; every person that leaves the palace is searched and examined, lest it should turn out to be my lady in disguise; at the least attempt at violence or escape I am to call them in; they are even now on the watch. There is not one of them that would dare to let you go; their punishment would be the most dreadful tortures you can imagine. You must be quiet, lady, and submit to the will of Alla—it is destiny. There, it is late—go to sleep; I will not disturb you.'

'And did you say he was coming here? When will he come here?—to-night?'

'No, no, not to-night,' replied the old hag, shaking her head—'not to-night.'

'To-morrow?'

'No, not to-morrow. You see, lady, he has

gone to fight the kaffirs, and when he has slain them then he will come.'

'May Alla grant that the kaffirs slay him,' said Leila. 'Then he will not come till he has effected their destruction?'

'No.'

'And that cannot be to-night?'

'No, for they do not begin the battle till to-morrow, and then perhaps he may not win it, for Alla does not always give the battle to the strongest.'

There was a reprieve at any rate, thought Leila; it will give me time to think. Depressed and heart-broken as she was, she had not lost all self-dependence yet. Her spirit was still strong, and her confidence in her own powers still unshaken. She resolved to assume a feigned calmness and composure, with a view to gaining leisure to think well over her circumstances and devise some plan for escape. So she kept up the conversation for some time longer, in order to ingratiate herself as much as possible with her unbidden guest, and keep her in a good humour, and then intimated her intention of retiring to rest, pleading fatigue. She refused to allow the old hag to summon her attendants, and refused still more plainly any assistance from her; but, unrobing herself with her own hands, she lay down on her couch, keeping up the conversation in a friendly conciliatory tone all the time, till at last, pretending to compose herself to sleep, she set to work to think over her situation, and look at it from all possible points of view to see if there was a gleam of hope from any side.

The old hag, too, after courteously enough, for her, wishing Leila good night, stretched her withered limbs upon the floor in her corner, from which she had never moved more than a pace or two, and both relapsed into silence—both feigning sleep. After an hour had passed, Leila, whose intellect and reasoning powers were more awake than they had ever been in her life before, ventured to raise her head very softly from the pillow, and looked through her half-closed eyelids at the figure of the watcher in the corner. She seemed fast asleep, breathing calmly and regularly. Leila ventured to raise her head a little more, and look round: the light was burning low in the room—there was no sound in the palace—all seemed hushed and still—nothing but the calm steady breathing of the old woman was there to break the solemn stillness of the midnight hour.

Now, thought Leila, she must be asleep; I will wait a little, and then, if I can get up and put out the light, I shall have an advantage over her at any rate, for it is impossible she should be so well acquainted with these apartments as I am; if she awake she will lose herself in the dark. And if she awake and make a noise——a thought came across her mind—a passing thought—but it made her shudder. Instinctively she felt for the little deadly weapon *he* had given her, whose point, laden with poison, would in one moment put her beyond the reach of him or any other mortal, and might with equal ease put the old hag, or any other living being that stood between her and freedom, beyond power of working her ill. She rose gently with the idea of getting up to extinguish the light. The delicate fabric of her night-dress made the slightest rustling in the world, hardly enough to disturb a mouse, yet in an instant she saw, with horror no words can describe, the little glistening black eyes of the old hag peeping forth from between the now raised eyelids: she was too watchful.

'I must wait,' thought Leila, 'till she goes to sleep;' and she did wait, and watched and watched through the long silent night hour after hour, yet whenever she made the slightest movement that little basilisk eye was upon her in a moment. At last Leila herself began to feel drowsy. Lying with the eyes almost closed, in a room where the feeble light of a solitary night-lamp scarce serves to break the gloom, in perfect stillness and silence, broken only by the regular breathing of another sleeper, especially when the bodily frame is wearied and worn out with fatigue, and the mind feels the reaction that follows upon intense emotion, it is very difficult to keep awake. Certainly Leila allowed herself to doze. Then you might have seen the little black eye of the old hag open and take a good look at the sleeper. Then she moved ever so gently, and watched. Leila lay perfectly still and motionless. She moved again, again, with like result. Then, softly divesting herself of her loose upper robe, leaving her arms and neck bare, the old woman for the first time since she had entered the room left her corner, creeping on all fours like a cat. She crept all round to where Leila kept the stock of medicaments and charms, and filters and vials and medicines she set such store by, softly opened the box—so softly as scarce to disturb a fly upon the lid—and took out bottle after bottle, testing their contents by the smell, and replacing each till she came upon the one she wanted. Then she crept round to Leila's couch. The beautiful sleeper lay, with her arms and breast uncovered, her head thrown back upon the pillow, slightly turned away from the light. The old hag's movements now became more speedy, though equally silent and stealthy as before. She took a handkerchief and drenched it with the fluid in the bottle; then, raising her arm, suddenly covered the mouth and nose of the sleeper with the handkerchief, holding Leila's hands with her other hand at the same time, by way of precaution. It was needless; the drug took instantaneous effect, and the sleeper lay motionless, deprived of sense and will, and at the mercy of her conqueror. She then got up from her crouching position, examined Leila's dress carefully, and took from her the poisoned stiletto. There was nothing else about her person that was capable of being made use of as a weapon either against herself or others. She then went to the box, took out the bottles and packets of powder, and scattered and spilt their contents upon the ground. All this occupied but a very short time indeed. She then returned to Leila, took the handkerchief from her mouth, and retired to her own corner, where she lay down exactly in her former position.

By-and-by Leila began to recover consciousness: she moved, raised her head, putting her hand up to it at the same moment, as if in suffering. The first thing that seemed to strike her was the strange odour in the room: she sniffed and sniffed again, then sat upright, and looked more intently at everything round her, and at the old woman feigning sleep. She then arose, and, divining at once the source whence the strange odour arose, went and examined the box. A glance at the contents upon the floor told the story at once, and there was her own handkerchief drenched with the liquid whose sense-destroying properties she knew so well. She put her hand into her bosom and felt for her stiletto; it was gone!

The old woman got up now and tried to raise Leila on to her couch, for she had fainted away.

CHAPTER LIV.

When Leila recovered she was much comforted to find that the old hag had relieved her of her presence. She was tended by her own female domestics, who behaved not, indeed, with respect, but with kindness. How time sped she neither knew nor cared. She ate and drank almost mechanically the food that was brought to her—sparingly enough indeed, but sufficiently to keep up the physical strength which she felt she might at any time need; not but what she often wished some of her domestics had been considerate enough to mix poison with her food, and so put an end to life and anxiety at once. She had aroused herself once to see how far she was a prisoner, and how far freedom was allowed her to come and go as she pleased, and soon learnt that in this respect she was no better off than before the visit of the old hag. She could not go beyond the precincts of her own apartment without being attended by female servants and eunuchs enough to overpower her by force at once if she attempted to make good her escape. Seeing the hopelessness of her position, she ceased to entertain any idea of attempting flight, and resigned herself to her fate, whatever that might be, with a blind trust in destiny, at the same time resolving to be on her guard and ready to take advantage of any circumstance that might turn up to operate in her favour.

The day following that on which the final assault on the fortified house took place, she was surprised by a sudden intimation, conveyed to her by a servant, that the Mirza intended to visit her that evening. She received the intelligence with apparent indifference; in reality, however, though unwilling to show it, she was considerably excited at the prospect of the interview. Intense as were the feelings of hatred with which she viewed this man, any change in their present relative position she thought must be for the better. Her past sufferings had given her confidence and moral strength, and she felt less afraid of meeting her oppressor now than she would have done some days before, ere the mask had been thrown off, and he had appeared in the character of her captor and her jailor. She prepared herself therefore for the coming interview with particular care, taking especial pains to add to her natural dignity of person those accompaniments which scrupulous attention to her dress and adornment could confer. 'If he is really passionately in love with me,' she thought, 'this is the only way I can hope to influence him or to obtain the slightest concession to my wishes.'

When he came, she received him with studied coldness and indifference. He was splendidly dressed, and his military accoutrements, his cuirass of polished steel, his green scarf, his handsome jewelled turban and arms with costly ornaments, set off his fine commanding person to the greatest advantage. His features, too, always handsome and gleaming with intelligence, were lit up with an expression of triumphant joy at the immediate prospect of success in his most cherished schemes of ambition. In his behaviour and address to the lady he professed to love with such adoring devotion he was most respectful and chivalrous. He knelt and kissed her hand as if he had been an accepted lover and she had smiled upon his suit. The occasion was an awkward one, for neither spoke for some little time, each being unwilling to give the other an advantage.

At last she broke the silence, which became more unbearable than the task of commanding her feelings sufficiently to address him.

'To what do I owe this visit?' she said.

'To my intense longing and desire to see you once again, lovely Leila, and to talk over our future plan, and to tell you of my success, and how I won it, and of the lofty position and dignity in store for you, and of the reward which Alla will give you for your faith and zeal.'

'And to give your captive liberty, I hope, too.'

'Yes, liberty. As the queen and mistress of him who now kneels before you, Leila—who will be to-morrow the greatest noble in the empire of Hindustan, second only to the vice-gerent of God himself.'

'Such a posture then befits not so great a dignitary. And pray, what of my husband? Am I to wed his murderer, or do you share by his consent a husband's rights?'

'Your husband, Leila, is he who stands, since you will not suffer him to kneel before you. The late Nawab—may the blessing of Alla rest on his tomb!—has gone to paradise, and is now wandering in the celestial groves with a troop of houris by his side.'

The effect of this abrupt announcement upon Leila was very different apparently from what the speaker expected. She simply disbelieved every word he said; it was her purpose, however, to dissemble.

'Nay, then, if my lord is indeed dead my hand is free, and on whom can I bestow it more worthily than on the champion of Islam? Yet, my lord, I would fain have liberty to come and go as I please.'

The Mirza hardly knew whether she was speaking in earnest or in satire. He ventured, however, to take her hand and cover it with kisses.

'That will do,' she said, withdrawing her hand peevishly. 'And now, ere we discuss our future plans, pray enlighten me somewhat upon the past—the steps by which you have mounted so rapidly to such a lofty pinnacle of glory. And I would also hear something of my deceased husband. He was ever kind and good and generous to me'—here her tears began to flow—'but his heart was small—he had not the soul to aspire to great things. May he rest in peace! And you, how have you accomplished all this? Have you defeated the kaffirs? I have heard constant firing for several days past. They seem to have fought well, and long. Doubtless it was in battle against the infidel my late lord obtained martyrdom?'

'It was: he fell by the sword of the accursed Nazarenes; but they are doomed now. I have hunted them to earth, and they cannot escape. They are shut in the bowels of the earth. Vain fools! they thought to deceive me; but I have them, and by to-morrow the men come forth to die, and the women and children to captivity.'

'And the beautiful lady that you persuaded me to decoy into your grasp, what of her?'

'She is destined, Leila, to the highest honour any living mortal can attain — an honour that even I could envy, were I of the other sex: she is to be your slave.'

'My slave! I am indeed grateful. I like her winning, gentle ways, and shall be glad to have her about me: but recollect, I shall be very jealous—Leila admits no rival.'

'Nay, do not remind me of that foolish passing passion; it was transient, as the cool breeze after a shower,—a mad, foolish passion, that but served to whet my appetite till I learnt to love you, Leila—to love you for the matchless power of your intellect, that raises you to the level of the angels, no less than your peerless beauty and your commanding grace and dignity of manner. It was a mere passing passion, but it is right the loveliest flowers should not bloom alone: therefore I will place near you, to tend you, and adorn your beautiful figure, and to wait upon your wants, this lovely kaffir girl; and her beauty, sparkling as it is, so much inferior to yours, shall but serve to enhance the majesty of your queenly charms: the moon shines only the more brightly from the neighbouring glimmer of the evening star.'

'But you have not told me how you accomplished all your deep designs, who aided you?'

'Alla. Thanks to your influence, my beautiful Leila, among the soldiers, they all obeyed my voice when I summoned them round the green standard: the money you sent them, and the many kind messages, and the feasts and presents, quite won their hearts and turned them into one channel like water; and when the brave old chief, Doonghur Rao——'

'Doonghur Rao! what, has he joined you?' asked Leila, speaking for the first time since the interview in her natural manner, and exhibiting no small alarm, for she thought of her husband, and the possibility of the story being really true, now that his old antagonist appeared as one of the actors in the drama.

'Yes, he joined heart and soul, and together we marched and besieged the infidels.'

'And it was in battle, you say, my late lord fell: was it open war, where man met man in fair and open fight?'

'It was; he fell, as I told you, by the sword of the infidel Nazarene.'

'Go on,' said Leila, apparently much relieved.

'I was saying, when Doonghur Rao joined us, our success was certain. The Nazarenes fought like devils—they always do—but they fell before the valour of the faithful, and the standard of Islam waves over the grave of the Christians. This night I complete my conquest, and to-morrow, Leila, will come to claim my reward.'

'To-morrow!—nay, that is too soon. The customs of our ancestors, and the tenets of our common faith, are not thus lightly to be set aside. For a prince in Islam, the second to the vicegerent of Alla on the throne of the Moghuls, the chosen of God, the favourite of the Prophet, yourself a sacred instrument in the hand of the Almighty for the destruction of the infidel—you would not take to your throne and to your bed one impure, who has not observed the hundred days of mourning enjoined by our holy book. Nay, let these rites be duly paid to the memory of him who has now gone to his reward; and then—then Leila will be his for whom she is destined.'

'Thanks, dearest Leila, for this promise; a thousand times thanks'

She gently but firmly repulsed the rather

too profuse expressions of his gratitude, and warned him by an angry look that as yet she was not his. She suffered him to kiss her hand again, and then withdrawing it, as if to bring the interview to a close, she said—

'And now, my lord, be good enough to bid the domestics in the palace pay me a little more respect than they have done lately. Your professions of devotion and humility are little worth, if you suffer her whom you pretend to worship with such adoration to be a laughing-stock for menial servants. Nay, I do not want to allude to the past,' she went on, by a gesture interrupting him, as he was about to ask forgiveness for the rude, harsh treatment she had been subjected to; 'I will not allude to the past, though I well might, and heap reproach upon reproach for the insults heaped on me, for the days and nights of suffering, the infamous treatment I have been subjected to, by your orders; a goodly augury for the future, truly!'

'Pardon me, Leila,' he said, interrupting her; 'pardon the too harsh expression of my intense, my anxious love. A treasure that we value above all price, above life itself, do we not guard with most jealous care? I knew well your high spirit, your excitable feelings, your daring aspirations. I knew nothing would keep you from rushing to the side of your adored husband, and remaining there in the thickest of the fight, or searching for his body among the slain, where the bullets fell like hail. I feared that, when the intelligence reached you of his unhappy death, nothing would prevent you from severing with your own hand the thread of life, the means of doing which, in so many ways, all easy and painless, I had myself taught you. I knew all this; I felt and saw that the only way of securing the precious prize was to watch it night and day. I would not, I dared not leave the field myself, or I would have come and with my own lips persuaded you to give me up those too dangerous weapons I had myself given you. I was helpless. All I could do was to watch you with trustworthy eyes day and night, till these things could be taken out of your way. The instant that was done, Leila, you were relieved of the presence of the old woman, whom, believe me, I only sent here from necessity.'

'You have my best thanks for your great consideration, my lord; and now, to complete your goodness, be so kind as to summon my domestics, and give them charge in my presence that I am mistress here; and also order a litter to be in attendance: I will go out; I have been too long a prisoner, and need fresh air.'

Leila had a way of showing she meant what she said, and the Mirza saw it was useless to attempt delaying compliance with her wishes, unless he was to throw off the mask altogether, and subject her again to actual coercion and restraint. He intimated acquiescence, accordingly, with her wish; and, summoning an attendant, desired him to bid Sidi Gulzar to assemble the whole household.

The eunuch stared when he mentioned Sidi Gulzar's name, and, after some hesitation, the order having been repeated, he replied that Sidi Gulzar had not been seen for some days, not since the Nawab had left the palace, and it was supposed he had gone with his old master.

The Mirza turned to Leila for some explanation, but she was unable to offer any. He then directed all the household to be summoned in the court-yard below, where he could speak to them, while Leila, from the lattice of her room, which looked out on the court-yard, could hear all he said. He then took his leave with many protestations of his undying passion, and a promise to have a litter and a guard of honour at Leila's disposal immediately.

He then descended to the court-yard, where he addressed a few authoritative words to the assembled household, warning them that any-one who exhibited the slightest disrespect to the mistress of the palace, either by word or deed, should pay the penalty of death, and then enquired where Sidi Gulzar was. For a long time all the servants stoutly denied having seen anything at all of him, and it was likely enough they spoke the truth, for the men who had placed him in confinement had left the palace, and were with the Nawab's retinue in camp. The man to whom the Nawab had, however, given the order to take the prisoner food was there; and after a great deal of questioning had gone on, and each one had been examined separately, he came for-ward and confessed that he had received the Nawab's orders, but had fairly forgotten to execute them, and from that time he had never so much as thought of the existence of the chief eunuch, amid the stir of so many exciting events.

Full of misgivings as to his fate, the Mirza hastened to the place indicated as the locality in which the prisoner had been confined. It was a little room in a turret at one angle of the palace, exposed to the rays of the sun in such a way as to be at this time of the year more like a little oven than an abode fit for a human being. It was closed on all sides, there being only one door, and that was locked. The Mirza shook it, knocked, called, but no answer came. He then told them to bring something to knock in the door with, and a light. He snatched the torch from the hand of the attendant who brought it; and as the door fell beneath the stroke of the hammer, he crossed the threshold and entered.

The atmosphere of the cell, for a cell it was, was not such as to tempt one to remain, nor was the sight that met the Mirza's eyes a pleasant one. There lay the old eunuch, in one corner, a mass of corruption—the heat and the deprivation of food and water had done their work—he must have been dead at least some days.

The Mirza came out, pale with rage and the sickening effect of the impure air.

'Bring that man here,' he said.

They dragged forward the culprit who had confessed to receiving orders to supply the prisoner with food.

'Look at your handiwork, sirrah!' he cried. 'In with him—he shall keep the old man company.'

The servants were horror-struck at the sentence: they hesitated. He repeated the order in a tone that showed he meant to be obeyed. The doomed wretch threw himself at his feet, and implored pardon in the most piteous accents. The Mirza was deaf to all entreaties.

'In with him!' he cried; and recollecting that the door was broken down, added, 'And send for bricks and mortar, do ye hear, and wall it up. Two of you remain, and take care that the murderer comes not forth.'

This act of severe retributive justice having been completed, the Mirza left the palace, mounted his horse, and rode forth, accompanied by his escort, towards the city. He had ordered a levy of five thousand able-bodied men to be assembled for some work he had in store for them, and went to see that his orders had been carried out. He found them all drawn up in the plain where the camp had been pitched. From thence they were marched off to the site of the ruined house, and employed in removing the débris that had accumulated by the fall of the broken walls. They worked with a will, for there were overseers directing them, who had orders to see that the whole was removed before the dawn of the ensuing day.

CHAPTER LV.

'Do you know the road here, Graham? It is difficult to find. There is a large village in front—it would be as well to get round somehow if we can—we shall only create a panic if we go through,' said a voice in the darkness.

'Yes, I know the way; follow me,' said Graham, urging his horse to the front—he had been riding behind the first speaker.

'Tell them to close up behind there,' called out a third.

'Ay, ay, sir,' was the rejoinder from a fourth.

There was a great clattering of hoofs and neighing of horses, and jingling of steel appointments, as the cavalcade made the best of its way along a narrow winding lane, flanked by tall hedges of cactus, or the prickly pear, that grows in such profusion in many parts of India. The road passed close outside a walled village, and in spite of their efforts not to disturb the inhabitants, the dogs very soon began to give tongue as the advance of the party disturbed them. One after the other took up the chorus, till there was such a barking, yelling, and howling, you could scarce hear a man speak. The watchmen of the village speedily gave the alarm, and one by one the inhabitants left their houses and peered over the walls to see the cause of this uproar. There was very soon a regular panic in the place, for it was whispered from mouth to mouth that an armed party were approaching. Many of the villagers began to bury the most valuable part of their property; women stripped off their ornaments hastily and threw them to their frightened husbands, who grubbed up the earth in the corner of the huts, like dogs; others fairly took to their heels, and did not stop running till they had got into the open fields; others again, more venturesome than their neighbours, stayed upon the walls to see with their own eyes what the danger was before they ran away from it. By-and-by the consoling intelligence reached them that the Feringhees, or dacoits, or whatever they were, had turned off, and were not coming to the village at all; then they mustered courage to creep out into the open ground and peer through the cactus hedges, behind which they could lie concealed in the darkness without a chance of being observed. Those who ventured thus far were gratified by seeing the party whose approach had caused such consternation pass along the lane without exhibiting the slightest symptoms of any hostile or marauding intent.

It is time, however, that I described this party, and who composed it. First of all rode Graham in advance to show the way. Two horsemen riding abreast followed close behind him. They were well mounted; their steeds were not by any means so fresh, though, as they had been three or four days before—a succession of forced marches in the hot weather is wearing both to man and beast. Sir Marmaduke Mastodon's iron constitution, however, bore it well enough, and so did Mr. Bowlemover's, for these were the two horsemen: the latter, indeed, suffered a great deal more from fatigue than his companion, as he was less accustomed to it, but his old tastes acquired in his younger sporting days soon returned, and the novelty and excitement of the work they had in hand compensated for the lack of youthful vigour that had declined with advancing years.

After them, came a party of fifty of Tupper's volunteer cavalry from Aurungabad, and a number of railway engineers and surveyors, indigo-planters and their assistants. The road was so narrow that they could only ride two and two abreast, so it took a long time for the whole party to defile by the village. After the volunteer cavalry, came a party of eighty men of H. M.'s 159th Foot, transformed into a mounted force, and riding upon camels: each soldier carried his rifle and ammunition, and the camel he rode was driven by a Sikh soldier, who sat in front and guided the animal—an arrangement carried out by Sir Marmaduke Mastodon when he passed through Aurungabad, not without difficulty, however, for Colonel Knickerbocker was so horrified at such an infringement of the usages of the service, and such an irregular way of disposing of infantry soldiers, that, on finding himself forced to yield the point, he took to his bed, and was not seen upon parade for a month afterwards; while Brigadier Littlesole, on having his garrison so much diminished, issued a brigade order directing the commissary of ordnance and chief engineer to make arrangements for mining the fort, and placing the necessary supply of powder in such a position that the whole place might be blown up at a moment's notice. He was determined, he said, to die at his post; and the only thing that consoled him in the gloomy prospect, was that he would blow up the civilians too.

Behind them came a party of a hundred and fifty Sikh irregular cavalry—Sir Marmaduke Mastodon's chosen escort, tried and faithful servants, and ready for any service. The whole force wended their way along in silence, for they had marched all night, and, as it was now nearly dawn, both man and beast were sleepy and tired.

'What time is it, Bowlemover? I'm feeling very sleepy; it must be near daylight, surely?'

'Yes, we shall have daylight before an hour. As for feeling sleepy, my dear fellow, don't think of such a thing. For my part, I could not think of sleeping if I was in a feather-bed, with curtains drawn all round, in England: sleeping's vulgar, I'm beginning to think.'

'Don't talk of feather-beds, for mercy's sake, man. Feather-beds and curtains! Pooh, think of a glass of iced soda-water and a plunge into the Nynee Tal lake.—Hallo, Graham! Do you know where we are? I am beginning to think you've lost your way, or that there's no such place as Islamabad at all: here have we been going it for the last six nights. Do you recollect this place?'

'Yes, well; I've been out here shooting before now; we have not got more than eight miles more. Do you know, Bowlemover, I am dreadfully anxious,' he added, reining up his horse and allowing the two to come up to him, for the road here widened, or rather disappeared altogether, leaving them to make their way across the fields, 'now that we are so near the end!—what if the worst has happened?'

Don't think of it; I'll bet ten to one Dacres has held out. But if we are so near the end of our journey, we had better fix what to do when we get there,—hadn't we, Mastodon?'

'By all means—a council of war! But councils of war never fight, I believe; and that won't do for us. I think we understand all about the position we are likely to find them in,—don't you, Bowlemover?'

'Oh yes; I have a general idea of the localities, of course, from what Graham has told us; but I do not think we can determine any course of action till we arrive at the spot and can see our ground.'

'Oh, we will take care to reconnoitre before we go into action. That sounds grand, doesn't it!—"go into action." I say, do you recollect Blunt?'

'What, the political, down at Indurpore when the war broke out?'

'Yes: well, he used to call every skirmish he had with his sowars an action. He came into my tent one day to breakfast—a late breakfast, about three o'clock in the afternoon—we had been out with the old chief reconnoitring, but, before we joined him, there had been a little skirmishing between our escort and some of the enemy's sowars. When he came into my tent, he said, "Mastodon, we've fought seven actions to-day." Pretty well that, for a morning's work before breakfast, wasn't it?'

'But, look here,' said Bowlemover, 'if they have all taken up their position in the tomb, as Graham says is most likely, we shall find the place surrounded.'

'I beg your pardon; this is a mere surmise of yours, my dear friend. We don't know yet that there is any enemy at all to oppose us.'

'You believe, then, the Nawab has been faithful?'

'I think it not impossible—at any rate, we need not make up our minds to fight till we know for certain there is an enemy to fight with. When I talked of going into action, I was only joking. I hope we shall find them all right, and have no more difficult duty to perform than to bring away the ladies and children. Eh, Graham, what say you?'

'Why, I know that before I left Dacres had no idea they would remain unmolested. It was, in his opinion, merely a question of time, as old Brigadier Littlesole says: besides, if the information we got at that village yesterday is to be depended on, there has been a good deal of fighting, with what result God only knows.'

'Well, we shall soon see.'

'Hallo! I recollect this large tree!' said Graham, after a short pause, during which they rode by a large peepul tree that stretched its branches half-way across the road. 'We can't be far from Chunderbagh now. When I said that village was eight miles, I meant eight miles to Islamabad. We must be close to Chunderbagh. Would it not be as well to halt and reconnoitre?'

'Perhaps it would. Is not that the first streak of dawn?'

'Yes, I think so.'

'Let us get the men together. Where is Captain Evans?—oh, he's gone back to see after his detachment. We'll halt your Cutchery hussars, or whatever you call them, Bowlemover, and let us wait till the rear comes up.'

Bowlemover gave the necessary orders, and

his volunteer troop formed up in a sort of line and dismounted. The whole detachment was well together; and they did not take long in assembling. Meantime the faint streak of dawn on the horizon became brighter and brighter, till daylight appeared.

Sir Marmaduke Mastodon had thrown himself on his back on the ground, holding his horse's reins with one hand; Bowlemover and Graham had just dismounted, and were both stretching themselves and yawning. Suddenly Mastodon started to his feet, and the other two jumped into their saddles. It was the report of cannon-shot almost close to them that caused this sudden movement. Graham was no coward, but his heart beat as if it would fly up into his mouth.

There was a great deal of excitement, but no confusion. The volunteers mounted; the company of the 159th remained seated on their camels; the Sikh troopers came to the front.

'Now, look here,' said Sir Marmaduke. 'Graham and I will go and reconnoitre; you had better come on cautiously, Bowlemover; and I think, Captain Evans, you had better dismount your men—they will be more useful on foot. But we cannot tell what to be at till we have seen what is going on. Those guns are shotted—eh, Graham?'

'Yes, I should say so; and, hark, there is a discharge of small arms: they are at it, hammer and tongs. For heaven's sake, come on!'

Followed by half-a-dozen of the Sikh horsemen, Sir Marmaduke and Graham cantered to the front; the remainder of the detachment advanced as had been directed. The first thing they saw when they got close enough to distinguish objects was a large mass of ruins, which on the side nearest them rose up in a high heap or hillock, in places obscuring from view everything that lay beyond. Over this ridge, formed by the débris of the house, the figures of armed men could be distinctly seen, climbing up to the summit, and then leaping down the other side, when they became lost to view. There was an immense body of them, and they disappeared by twos and threes in this manner, and could not be seen returning. On the right, between the two officers and the ruined dwelling, was a large dense crowd of unarmed men, coolies apparently, some standing, some sitting on the ground, but none of them actively engaged in any duty. Beyond and to the left and right the ground, as I have elsewhere said, descended to the lower level, upon which the tomb of the old Saiyad was built. From where Sir Marmaduke Mastodon and Graham stood, however, the depression of the level was sufficiently gradual to allow of their taking in at one glance pretty nearly the whole space beyond the site of the house and the tomb, and the plain that stretched away to the left and front. This was swarming with a sea of heads, all in motion. In one place a battery of guns kept up a perpetual discharge, while crowds of foot-soldiers poured a heavy matchlock and musketry fire on the same point, doubtless the doorway of the tomb, though this could not be distinguished from the point of view from which I am endeavouring to describe the scene as it presented itself to Graham and his friends. It was evident that the position on which the attack was being made was held, and that gallantly too; for every now and then the surging mass of heads that moved towards it was seen suddenly to surge back. At the same moment, volumes of smoke from the point evidently held by the defenders against the assailants showed that they reserved their fire, and gave it when it could be given with effect. The stream of men, however, still kept pouring up and over the heap of ruins, and this filled Graham with misgivings; for he could not at first conceive what their object was, or where they disappeared to behind that ridge of stones.

Sir Marmaduke Mastodon, who by common consent had assumed the generalship of the little party, had left Graham, for by this time the whole detachment had come up, and was pointing out to Captain Evans the direction in which he thought it most advisable for him to lead his men, now thrown out in skirmishing order. Bowlemover was on horseback by Graham's side; the volunteer cavalry drawn up immediately in rear, with swords drawn all ready for action. Suddenly Graham's attention became riveted on the host of combatants before him. A great movement had taken place: the firing ceased; in place of it, a shout, like the shout of victory and triumph, swelled to heaven from thousands of throats. At once the sea of heads surged backwards and forwards; there was a rush and a struggle, but it was impossible to make out anything with certainty. Graham's impatience was beyond control.

'If you won't come on, I'll go alone,' he said, turning to Bowlemover.

'Move on, move on, and charge when you think your ground clear and your distance right,' roared Sir Marmaduke, who had accompanied the skirmishers to a spot of ground a little elevated, about two hundred yards to the right front of where the volunteers were standing.

'Come along,' called Bowlemover, waving his hog-spear, in utter contempt of all military words of command.

They advanced at a trot for some distance, when the confused mass of struggling humanity resolved itself into something more definite. There was a movement out of and from the tomb, and a figure on horseback could now be discerned forcing his way through the crowd: he was clad in a cuirass of steel and wore a green scarf across his breast, while seated on his horse in front of him was a female form, whose loose drapery floated in the breeze as he bore her along. By-and-by—for his progress was impeded by the crowd through which he had to make his way—he was overtaken by a man on foot waving a naked sword: he seized the horse's bridle and forced the animal back on his haunches. A desperate hand-to-hand conflict now ensued between the two, desperate—for the horseman was encumbered with his burden, besides having to hold his reins. He was not unassisted, however, and the crowd of combatants rushed upon the assailants from all sides. And now came help; for two more men on foot staggered up and engaged in the unequal conflict—

now unequal, for there was a multitude against three.

All this, and a very great deal more which it would take me too long to describe, had been seen by Graham as he galloped towards the spot, followed closely by Bowlemover and the volunteers, and a hundred of the Sikh horsemen, waving their swords and shouting the Sikh war-cry, 'Gooroo Ji-ke-Futteh!' O that their horses' legs were wings, or that they could clear the ground like lightning!

'On, for God's sake,' cried Graham—'we shall be too late.'

He had recognised the figure in the grasp of the horseman with the steel cuirass and the green scarf.

Down the declivity they came, gaining impetus at every stride their horses took, who were as impatient to dash into the strife as their riders, and like an avalanche they hurled themselves upon the crowd: right and left went the gleaming sword-blades to cut a passage through that living mass. As for Bowlemover's hog-spear, it was worse than useless in the *mêlée*: they were at too close quarters for spears; but he used the butt-end, laden as it was with a heavy knob of iron, right lustily, and many a cranium would have cracked that day under it, had it not been they were so well protected by turbans. Still it did its work, for no man who got the iron knob of the spear wielded with all the force of Bowlemover's arm upon his head, though it was protected by folds of cloth, felt inclined to try it a second time.

The fierce and determined onset of so strong a body of men as the volunteers and the Sikhs produced very soon a wonderful effect. Many a head was turned from many quarters to see what was the cause of this sudden pressure from the flank; while at the same moment conical rifle-bullets came whizzing from the rear of the tomb in quick succession, each little ball laying low at least one out of that dense crowd. All this seems a long business to write—it may seem as long to read: in action it was, at least it seemed to the actors, like a lightning-flash. Blood flowed freely; the shower of rifle hail came pattering thick and deadly. On sped the cavalry, still charging at full speed, their sword-blades still gleaming as they struck, first on this side, then on that, till another shout was raised from that tumultuous crowd to heaven—this time it was a shout of panic; then followed such a scene that it is folly attempting to describe. There was a confused agonised yell of *fear*, and the whole mass surged and shook, and attempted by a common impulse to fly. Fly! in such a mass!—they only trod and trampled one another down. Meantime Graham has neared the little group from which his eyes have never once been taken. Burleigh—for it was he who held the horseman's bridle-rein—still struggles; his two comrades have been struck down; and just as Graham's sword waves above the Mirza's head, the sabre of the latter sweeps down with a back-handed stroke upon Burleigh's unprotected face; it cleft his head in two, and he fell at once.

The battle was well-nigh over now; the enemy were in flight, hard pressed by the victors. Up came Captain Evans's party, no longer skirmishing, but in line, charging the flying foe and bayoneting right and left. The Sikh horsemen and the volunteers spread out into line too; and Bowlemover, no longer closely pressed, and able to use his spear, rode at their head, and drove the enemy from the field, slaughtering as they went along. The Mirza had fallen badly wounded from his horse, but not before Graham had dismounted and caught in his arms the prize he was bearing off, when vengeance overtook him. Amy Leslie bore up against all; the terror of her situation was too extreme for her to be relieved even by swooning, till the moment when deliverance was at hand. Her eye suddenly rested on the pale, care-worn, haggard, yet well-remembered face of him she loved dearer than her life, and whom she believed long ago dead. At the moment she fancied her own death-hour had arrived, and that he had suddenly appeared from the world of spirits to accompany her to her long home. Then nature gave way; and, with a shriek of terror that rang in Graham's ears for days afterwards, she fell senseless on his breast.

CHAPTER LVI.

THE sun had set upon that blood-stained battle-field, as upon many a bloodier field both before and since. The combatants had disappeared. It was no longer a scene of deadly strife—the arena where man contended with savage ferocity against his fellow. It was deserted now—deserted by all but those who never desert the battle-field—the dead, the dying, the jackal, and the carrion-birds, and those human vultures more heartless than the beasts that prey upon the dead, who hang upon the skirt of war's 'red genius,' and strip the wounded and the dying.

The slaughter had been great in proportion to the small number engaged in actual conflict. But innumerable casualties had resulted, at any rate in the first instance, from the dense mass itself collected in that plain, all bent on the destruction of the gallant little band that kept them at bay so long, and little dreaming that their own discomfiture was at hand.

Panic-stricken by the sudden charge of the volunteer cavalry and Sikhs, the confusion that seized them was proportionate to the number of the crowd. Anything like an orderly retreat was out of the question; it was not attempted; all they thought of was flight. The flight of a mass of human beings, closely crowded together, even across a spacious plain, must be a fatal movement to many. The attempt was madness; the result, the destruction of hundreds. Numbers fell, and those who fell were trodden and trampled to death almost instantaneously. They shrieked, but none heeded their shrieks; the avenger was upon them, and their comrades thought only of their own safety. The spectacle presented by a battle-field, after an action, is never anything but horrible. On this occasion, however, the terrible aspect of the dead was such that it impressed the minds of those who saw it, though inured to all the horrors of war by long practice and bitter experience, with a sickening horror they never felt before. The bodies of those who had fallen were mangled in the most fearful way; trampled to death by the feet of the flying crowd, their limbs broken, their features in most cases destroyed beyond all power of recognition, and subsequently cut up by the lances and swords of the pursuing cavalry and the horses' hoofs, there was scarce a single body there that was not covered with frightful wounds, any one of which was enough to destroy life. The cavalry had swept through them, using their swords and lances freely, and without the slightest pity for the terror-stricken fugitives, who ran, or tried to run, like sheep; and those who, mangled and wounded, escaped death from the violence of their own flying comrades and the swords of the cavalry, were nearly all bayoneted by the infantry, who came up very soon after the cavalry had swept the field. The pursuit was not kept up beyond the outskirts of the city, in the suburbs of which the surviving fugitives found a temporary asylum; and on their return the Sikhs again swept the field, and put to death, often with revolting cruelty, and always with taunt and insult, the few they found in whose bodies the breath of life still lingered. Long before sunset, however, all active operations were over. The surviving ladies and children—alas! there were now but few!—were removed to the dawk bungalow, in the neighbourhood of which some of the tents belonging to the chiefs were found pitched, and in them and in the house they took up their abode. Ah! who shall describe the heartfelt fervour of the thanksgiving which arose that night from the hearts and lips of the little band, thus delivered in their greatest hour of need, to the throne of Him whose eye had been upon them all through their period of suffering! One, however, was absent—he to whom, under Providence, they all owed their lives. Where was Dacres?

Cool and collected in the midst of the battle, Dacres had observed how things were going on from the first. So vigorous was the attack, and so determined, and so overwhelming was the force engaged against them, that he despaired of success even from the commencement of the fight. It might, indeed, be possible to resist the tremendous onslaught on their little garrison for a time; they might be able to keep their enemies at bay, perhaps, till evening, but the odds were too great for them to hope for ultimate success. A few hours of such exertion as they were all called upon to undergo must of necessity wear out their vital powers, even if swords and cannon-shot spared their lives.

He had observed the Nawab seated on horseback at a great distance from the front, where the most active operations were going on, apparently taking no part in the battle, but regarding it as a spectator. He was surrounded by a posse of armed horsemen, and Dacres easily divined he was not his own master. As long as the battle was against them, the Nawab remained in the field; but the moment the tide turned, and the volunteers were seen charging to the rescue, the Nawab, now deserted by his escort or guard, instead of hastening to join his friends, turned his horse's head, and fled from the field in the direction of the city. Dacres saw him ride off, and it struck him at the time as most singular; but he had many other things to think of, and in the hurry of the engagement, and press of business that immediately followed, he forgot all about the Nawab's hasty flight. As soon as all was over, and he had leisure to reflect on his next course of action, the strange behaviour of the Nawab immediately recurred to him, and after a hasty meal he mounted a horse belonging to one of the relieving force, and, accompanied by a few of the Sikh escort, rode off to the city, partly with a view of seeing what was going on there, and whether the rebels had any intention of making another stand, and partly to find out and confer with the Nawab as to their future course of operations, which it was all-important should be carried out with vigour, judgment, and decision.

The road the whole way almost to the city he found strewed with melancholy relics of the late fight: men wounded, dying, and dead, lay at intervals in the middle of the road, where they had been struck down, or in the ditches on either side, whither they had crawled to die.

The city was in the utmost confusion. The troops—or at least the men who had borne arms and been professedly engaged in the late fight—afraid of being followed up by the overwhelming British force which they believed was behind them, had dispersed and concealed themselves—some in obscure parts of the city, and some in the gardens and suburbs beyond. The wealthy traders, the merchants and shopkeepers, fearful of seeing the city sacked by a host of European soldiers, buried their choicest valuables, and made their escape out of the place with as much of the remainder of their property as they could carry, taking their wives and children with them. The narrow streets were in consequence absolutely blocked up by the crowd of panic-stricken fugitives, and Dacres could only with the utmost difficulty make his way through them. The day before, had he shown himself there, his life would have been sacrificed without a doubt; but to-day he rode unmolested, not even insulted, along the most densely-populated streets, forcing his horse through the crowd of foot-passengers. His progress was slow and tedious, and the sun had set before he emerged into the open country on the further side of the city. Here, finding no traces of the enormous band of armed men that had been arrayed against them, and making up his mind that they must have dispersed to their homes and would give no further annoyance, he turned and retraced his way to the city, and thence to the Nawab's palace. It was night when he reached it, but bright moonlight. The palace seemed to be in as great confusion as the city. There were a few attendants and loungers hanging about the gates, from whom he learnt on enquiry that the Nawab was within. He rode into the court-yard, gave his horse to one of his escort to hold, and entered the palace on foot, accompanied by three or four of his attendant Sikhs, on foot also. The interior of the palace seemed almost entirely deserted, but there were a few servants about. On enquiring from them where the Nawab was, they pointed in silence towards the seraglio, and thither, after in vain attempting to get anyone to go on and announce his arrival, Dacres proceeded.

Half afraid of intruding where he might not

be wanted, yet filled with anxious presentiment and foreboding, and at the same time most desirous of meeting the Nawab, with whom it was absolutely necessary he should gain a conference, he advanced cautiously and slowly, pausing at the threshold of each room, and listening carefully to find out if it was occupied or empty. There was no light to guide him, and never having been there before, he was utterly at a loss to know whither to direct his steps, or whither the corridor which he was now traversing would lead. At length he reached the threshold of an apartment which was certainly occupied by some living tenant, for he could distinctly hear a low sound of moaning, as from some one in deep grief or pain inside. He paused and listened, then cautiously drew aside the curtain and peeped in.

A flood of moonlight that poured through an open casement lit up the interior of the apartment. It was spacious, and handsomely built. The walls were beautifully decorated, being lined with snow-white marble, elegantly carved in the semi-Saracenic and semi-Italian style, so often seen in Mahometan buildings erected in the seventeenth century. The ceiling was curiously formed of innumerable polished mirrors of octagonal shape fitting one into another, each with a narrow framework of gold and silver filagree alternately, the whole in the form of a series of pointed domes, supported by rows of slender and profusely-ornamented pillars, all of white marble, and carved in elegant tracery. On the opposite side an arched doorway gave entrance to another apartment beyond, separated by a handsome red damask curtain, ornamented with silken ropes and tassels, that hung in ample folds from the ceiling to the ground. The moveable furniture of the room consisted of cushions of red and purple velvet, placed on the marble floor against the foot of the walls all round; while, in the centre, stood a couch or bed, half concealed by muslin drapery of the purest white, that glistened in the moonbeams like silver gauze. At the side of the bed, seated on the ground with the head buried in the drapery of the couch, was a figure, and from this figure proceeded the sounds of grief that had attracted Dacres's attention and arrested his step. This figure could be no one but the man he was in search of. He called the Nawab by name, at first softly, then more loudly, finding that his low tones failed to receive attention. At last he was successful; the figure moved, turned, and looked towards the intruder. On seeing who it was, he rose to his feet and advanced to the door to meet him. The Nawab, for it was he, spoke not a word, but taking Dacres's outstretched hand, led him in silence to the side of the bed, and pointed to it. There, with her angelic features lit up by the pale moonlight, themselves as white as the snowy drapery on which her form reposed, lay Leila, sleeping the sleep of death. Dacres paused and gazed in solemn silence on the scene. Solemn it was, but he thought he had never seen anything more beautiful. His companion stood beside him for a minute or two; then, as if the fountain of his heart had suddenly burst the icy bands of grief that had frozen it, threw himself on his knees, buried his face in the drapery again, and burst into a fit of weeping. Dacres, inured to scenes of trouble as he was, could scarce avoid the contagion of grief, and with difficulty suppressed his own tears. But he had come there to work for the living, not to weep over the dead. What could he do? He dared not intrude unbidden upon such an outpouring of sorrow with the cares of business and the concerns of active life. Still, time was precious, and time was passing. Again after a pause he addressed his heart-broken companion:—

'It is the will of God, Nawab—your highness must learn submission to the will of the Most High. She you love has already passed from the scene of her earthly troubles to the eternal rest of another world; we have been spared—have escaped great dangers, but great dangers surround us still. Your position, your fortune, your life demand immediate action. Could your tears restore to life that beautiful creature you love with such devotion, I would bid you weep till the fountain of your eyes were dried; but it is in vain. She has gone; know you how she met her death? Surely, it was calm and peaceful and painless: look at that beautiful expression on her face; she seems to smile upon you and to say, "Be comforted, for I am happy."'

'You speak well,' said the Nawab, rising and checking his unmanly burst of grief. 'She is gone; it is for me—for me to avenge her death!'

'Avenge?'

'Yes, avenge!—think you she died willingly? No; it was I who killed her, but another bears the guilt of this innocent life, and he shall suffer the punishment, as sure as Alla is One and Mahomet the prophet of God.'

'Do you know, then, how she met her death?'

'Alas! no; but this much I do know. When

forced away from my palace, and knowing that evil was before us both, and that my life and her honour were in the utmost jeopardy, and that the loss of one would be as the signal for the destruction of the other, I told her when the worst befel I would send her this ring—look how it still glistens on her finger!' and he stooped and passionately kissed the cold marble hand. 'And when the attack was made, and all thought it was final—for who expected that Alla had deliverance for us at hand?—I bribed the least untrustworthy of those who formed my guard (who had secret orders, as I knew, to slay me the moment the trumpet of that arch-fiend sounded out the note of victory)—I bribed him with a purse of gold to take this ring to her I loved dearer than life itself. Too well, too faithfully he fulfilled his fatal mission. Then, when the will of God in our deliverance was manifested and the sahibs charged upon our foes, my heart smote me as though a bullet from the kaffirs' guns had cleft it in twain. Swift as lightning, I sped from the field, in the hope that I might be in time to contradict my own messenger—alas! of death. I was too late: you see the rest.'

'But how has she accomplished the end? I see no sign—no fatal weapons—no wound—

no mark on her calm features of the convulsion caused by poison. How was it?'

'Alas! I know not. I found her thus—it was enough; what need I know more?'

'But let us satisfy ourselves on this point. Take off the covering, and see if she has any mark upon her person. I will turn away.'

He turned away as he spoke, and the Nawab, obedient as a child to the stronger will of his companion, proceeded to uncover and examine the corpse. Dacres moved mechanically towards the open lattice. As he approached it, something caught his eye, lying on the velvet cushion beneath the window, in the shade. He stooped down to examine it, rather with the view of giving himself some occupation, however trivial, than with any real intention or design.

The object he stooped to look at was a small basket with a lid. He lifted it to the open window, as he fancied something stirred inside; thinking, probably, it was some pet animal, belonging to the ill-fated occupant of the chamber. It was a living creature, but not of the kind Dacres thought to find: it was a small snake, beautiful in appearance, but so venomous that its bite was instant death. The thought flashed across his mind—'She must have been a second Cleopatra.'

As he stood at the window wrapt in thought, the basket with the dangerous occupant still in his hand, the Nawab approached him.

'The only mark I can find,' he said, 'is a small wound on the ankle of the right leg—a small wound such as might be made by a—— Alla! what is that?' he added, as the snake, disturbed from its lair, roused itself and thrust its head out between the little bars of the basket: then the truth flashed across his mind too, and with a cry of sorrow and despair he threw himself upon the bed.

Finding all his efforts to arouse the Nawab to the necessity for action vain, Dacres took from his unresisting hand his signet-ring, the seal of which was sufficient to attest his authority to any written orders or instruments, and leaving the heart-broken husband in the chamber of death, hurried out to take what measures he might deem expedient for restoring order in the city.

CHAPTER LVII.

Dacres was busy all that night in the Nawab's palace in the work of reorganisation. Next morning, however, at daybreak, he mounted his horse and rode out to Chunderbagh. As he neared the scene of the recent strife, he observed a crowd under a clump of trees, engaged in some very interesting work, apparently.

By-and-by one of the party saw him from a distance, and rode towards him, gesticulating in a most frantic manner, as if he was mad. Dacres put spurs to his horse and galloped on. He had not gone very far before he saw that it was Murray who was thus, by dumb show, beckoning him on. As Dacres approached he called out, for the latter was by this time within earshot,

'Make haste! make haste! here's a go!'

'What is it?' shouted Dacres, trying to overtake Murray, who had now turned his horse's head, and was galloping back to the clump of trees. Here, too, he continued his violent gesticulations, this time addressed to the little knot of persons gathered together under the trees; and by-and-by the rest of the crowd, who were all collected round something, what Dacres could not see, turned and looked towards him, as if awaiting his approach.

When he reached the spot, full of wonder and anxiety, he found Sir Marmaduke Mastodon seated on horseback, looking very stern: a number of his Sikh escort were there, too, all with their swords drawn, while in the centre of the group, right under the branch of a tree which extended in a horizontal direction some distance above their heads, was a bullock-cart or hackery. The bullocks, yoked, were standing with their faces in the opposite direction from that in which Dacres had approached, awaiting, as it appeared, the order of a bluff, burly-looking European who stood beside the cart. But, standing on the edge of the cart, with his hands securely tied behind him, the fatal noose round his neck fastened at the other end to the branch of the tree, stood—Thurston.

Dacres rubbed his eyes, and looked, then turned to Murray, then to Sir Marmaduke Mastodon, then to the Sikhs, and finally to Thurston himself, as if silently demanding explanation. All this was but a moment in actually passing, though it takes long to describe, for no sooner had Dacres ridden up than Thurston accosted him.

'I call you to witness, Dacres, this foul murder committed in the name of the law—a foul murder, and nothing else. I am innocent, so help me God—I am innocent of the charge for which I am to be hanged; but enquiry will be made into it, depend upon it, and the law of England will have revenge on the murderer!'

'What is all this?' gasped Dacres, as soon as he could speak.

'All what?' said Sir Marmaduke. 'Did you never see a man hanged before? I've got enough against this villain to hang twenty such wretches.'

'Pray stay one moment,' urged Dacres; 'let me hear—there may be some mistake.'

'Mistake! I tell you I have been hunting this fellow for the last month; for the last month I have been in possession of the most damning evidence against him.'

'It's false; it's all a lie—a monstrous, hideous lie—a mistake. Stop him, Dacres, stop him for mercy's sake; don't bring guilty blood on your soul. I am innocent—I am indeed—its some damned plot. Sir Marmaduke Mastodon is mad; do not let him commit himself. I adjure you, a British officer, will you stand quietly by and see such foul murder done? Cut him down!'

'Read this if you doubt the justice of this sentence,' said Sir Marmaduke, handing Dacres a roll of papers which he pulled out of his holsters. 'And you, sir, if you don't hold that tongue of yours, I'll have you gagged at once. I've hanged too many traitors and rebels lately to be bearded by such a villain as you.'

While Dacres is reading, and Thurston, cowed with fear, with difficulty swallowing his indignation, let us go back a little and recount briefly the manner in which the philanthropist came into such an ugly position.

The previous evening, the rest of the party having dispersed in different directions, he was making his way towards the travellers' bungalow, when he heard some one calling to him from behind. He stopped, and turning round, beheld an officer on horseback surrounded by a Sikh escort. The officer galloped up to him, and at once asked him if he went by the name of 'Thurston.' On his replying in the affirmative, Sir Marmaduke, for it was he, said, 'Then you are my prisoner,' and without another word made a sign to his men, saying something to them in Punjabee which Thurston could not understand. They, however, immediately surrounded him. Two of them dismounted, seized Thurston, put him on one of their horses, and rode away with him a close prisoner. Sir Marmaduke rode away also, but at such a distance that Thurston could not make him hear, though he called repeatedly to him. They took him to a large tent, where he was allowed to seat himself in a chair, two of the Sikhs, however, standing by him all the time with swords drawn. He sat there till it was dark. By-and-by Sir Marmaduke came in, accompanied by two other officers, Captain Evans and Mr. Bowlemover, who had been pointed out to him by name before, though, owing to the confusion they had been in, and the active duties they were all engaged in, he had not had an opportunity of speaking to either of them. Lights were brought, and the three officers seated themselves at the table, Sir Marmaduke in the centre. The latter unlocked a writing-box before him, and took out a bundle of papers. These he showed to Bowlemover, and while he was reading them, Thurston being seated on the opposite side of the table, Sir Marmaduke handed him a piece of paper and a pen, and desired him to write his name.

'Will you allow me to ask, gentlemen, the

meaning of this strange behaviour on your part,' he said; 'by what right you have arrested me in this way? I demand your authority, in the first place, for acting as you have done; and in the second, if you have authority to arrest me, I require to know the charges you have against me.'

'Here is my authority,' said Sir Marmaduke, handing Thurston a bundle of printed papers which he took out of a box before him. 'You will find it under the head "Notification Extraordinary;" an order of the Governor-General in Council, appointing me special commissioner, with full powers to proceed under Act 1785 of 1857, which you will also find there, to hold summary enquiry, investigation, and trial into all cases of rebellion and conspiracy in the Central Indian Provinces, and to pass sentence on offenders, and to carry out such sentence by summary process.'

'Rebellion! conspiracy! what has this to do with me? If you are jesting, gentlemen, allow me to tell you it is most ill-timed jesting. My name is Thurston; I am a gentleman of independent property, M.P. for Rottenborough. Here have I been fighting like a common soldier, exposed to the utmost privation and dangers every hour of the day and night since the mutiny first broke out, and you charge me with rebellion! Pray send to the commissioner, Mr. Dacres; I have been living with him;—send for Captain Murray, Mrs. Murray—any of the survivors—they all know me. This unwarrantable outrage I protest against, and will certainly sue you for damages, unless you mean it for a jest.'

'No jest, sir; you stand charged with aiding and abetting and instigating rebellion and murder, and I can tell you the proofs are damning; and as there is but one sentence, and that is death, I advise you to think of and advance any exculpatory circumstances you can. I have, at your request, shown you my authority for acting—a thing I was not bound to do: you see that I have authority to proceed with this case and adjudicate upon it alone; as it has, however, some important and peculiar features—such as the fact of the prisoner, yourself, passing yourself off, and not without some show of probability, as an Englishman—I am happy to have the opportunity of associating with myself in this investigation one of the judges of the highest court of judicature of these provinces, Mr. Bowlemover, who has kindly consented to share with me the responsibility of this investigation, and to aid me with his very valuable judicial experience and advice. I repeat it—

you stand charged with instigating, aiding, and abetting rebellion and murder. Will you have the goodness to take this pen and sign your name in your usual manner on this paper?'

'I have no objection to doing that much, certainly,' replied the astounded prisoner; 'but of all strange things I ever heard, this is the strangest.'

He took the paper and pen, and wrote his name as he was desired; then rubbed his eyes, as if doubtful whether he was really awake, or under the influence of some horrible dream or nightmare.

Sir Marmaduke took the signature, examined it carefully, then handed it to Bowlemover; they compared it with the writing at the foot of the document already before them, looked at one another, and nodded.

'No doubt about it,' said Bowlemover.

'Very well,' said Sir Marmaduke, taking up one of the papers before him and handing it across the table to the astonished Thurston.

He took the paper and looked at it. It was covered with writing in Persian, and at the foot was a seal, which Thurston recognised at once to be his own seal which he was in the habit of using, and signed by his own name, and, as it certainly appeared, in his own handwriting. Again he rubbed his eyes, and thought he must be dreaming. How came his seal and signature there?

'Is that your seal and signature?' asked Sir Marmaduke.

'It is certainly my seal, that is, the seal I ordinarily use, and it appears to be my signature. I should say it was my signature, except that I am ready to swear I never signed such a document as that.'

'Oh! perhaps you do not understand what is in this document bearing your seal and signature?' said Sir Marmaduke, with an ill-disguised sneer.

'Most certainly I do not.'

'Then listen. Do you acknowledge, or do you not, having written as follows? I will translate it literally, according to the English version that accompanied the document when it fell into my hands:—

'"To the Most Mighty and Awe-Inspiring Prince of the Seven Climes, the descendant of the most illustrious house of Timour, now seated on the throne of Delhi—greeting.

'"This is to inform your Serene Highness that the English people have for long viewed with regret and indignation the grievous oppression exercised by the unprincipled servants of the East India Company upon the inhabitants of Hindoostan. That Company, by means of unprincipled and aggressive policy, pursued for many years unchecked, have extended their power far beyond the legitimate limits formerly assigned to them by royal charter. The time has arrived when the overgrown fabric of their power should be thrown down; and the people of England would see with pride and pleasure the oppressed inhabitants of Hindoostan throw off the yoke of the usurper, especially if headed by any of the descendants of the ancient aristocracy of the country. Nor can there be any doubt of the success of such an undertaking. The native army is sufficiently powerful to assert the freedom of their countrymen, and to drive the usurper and the conqueror from their soil.

' "In the event of such an occurrence, there would be no assistance to be looked for from England. Before succour could arrive, the English in India might be annihilated; nor would England ever consent to risk the blood and treasure necessary for the reconquest of the country. On the contrary, she would witness with pride and satisfaction the re-establishment of the sovereignty of the descendants of the ancient rulers of Hindoostan; and Her Most Gracious Majesty the Queen would extend to any such ruler so installed in the possession of his hereditary right, the hand of brotherhood and alliance." '

During the reading of this paper Mr. Thurston first blushed, then turned pale, and then tried to force a sickly smile. Sir Marmaduke finished reading, and then looked enquiringly at the prisoner. As the latter remained silent, he asked him—

'Do you acknowledge the authorship of this document?'

'I must explain,' replied Thurston. 'I do acknowledge myself to be the author of it, but I deny that it was addressed to the person to whom the preamble dedicates it. The document is, indeed, an extract from a pamphlet written by me, but never published: it was intended for circulation in England. I deny that it was written with any treasonable intent, nor can I see how it can be so twisted as to bear any such interpretation. It was written in a language unknown to the people of India; nor can its contents have become known to them, unless it was translated, as it appears to have been done, by some one with treasonable intent.'

Sir Marmaduke nodded, and produced a second document like the first, signed and sealed in a similar manner.

'I have no English translation of this one,' he said, 'but will read it off as literally as I can. Listen—

'"The English public and the Great House of Assembly in Great Britain, sympathising deeply with the oppression undergone by the unhappy people of India at the hands of the servants of the Company, would under no circumstances send any English soldiers to assist the servants of the said Company in riveting the chains they have bound the people with, nor to defend their lives or those of their wives and children, should it please the Almighty to stir up the hearts of His creatures to effect their own deliverance by the destruction of the oppressors. By craft and dissimulation the East India Company have extended their empire; by craft and dissimulation have they set themselves to remove one by one the ancient customs of the people, which they have ever regarded with superstitious reverence, as they are indeed the bulwarks and outworks of their religion, which must sooner or later fall before the steady advance of Christianity. But the Almighty has placed a remedy in the hands of these people, and were they to rise unanimously against the enemies of their race and religion, and destroy them along with their wives and families, the latter would be only receiving the natural reward of their malpractices, and be deserving of their fate. The English people, who always sympathise with any race making an effort for their freedom, would not be backward to afford that sympathy to the Indian races struggling sword in hand to effect the deliverance of their country."

'What have you to say to this?' asked Sir Marmaduke, laying down the paper. 'Were you the author of this or not?'

'I do recognise it certainly as being an extract from a draft of a speech I wrote out, but never delivered—that is to say, with a few verbal alterations; but I repeat, as in the former case, the words can bear no treasonable interpretation as I used and intended to use them.'

'There is another,' said Sir Marmaduke, taking up a third and reading out:—

'"Proclamation issued to the faithful sons of Islam, in the city of Delhi, now in arms against the infidels:

'"Let not the faithful servants of the Most High, who have been stirred up to take just revenge by shedding the blood of their oppressors, and of those who would have used the sword and bayonet of the infidels to force them to eat the flesh of swine, and have polluted the Hindoo with the blood of the sacred cow, be plunged into the waters of affliction by the words of some of their holy men, that such deeds are distasteful to the Most High, and such as to anger the God of Heaven, and draw down upon them wrath and vengeance; for be it known that these intentions, which have been for many years hidden in the breasts of the infidel servants of the Company, have been patent to the enlightened and learned inhabitants of Europe, the Frank and the Russ; and the Emperors of these countries having communicated with the Empress of Inglistan (England), and expressed their abhorrence of such deceit and violence, the people of England have been made fully aware of these foul deeds and deceit of the Company, and are so enraged that these actions should be perpetrated in their name, that they have resolved to send their faithful and learned emissary by way of Iran (Persia) to the Court of the most illustrious Sovereign of the Seven Climes seated at the centre of the world, Delhi, to inform and instruct the people of that country of the horrible crimes that the servants of the Company are meditating against the oppressed subjects of the Emperor of Hindoostan; and to certify this the writer of this proclamation, whose seal and signature is affixed, has been deputed from Inglistan (England) to lay his humble petition at the threshold of the Court of the Emperor of the centre of Islam, the Light of the World, &c.

(Signed) '"T. THURSTON."'

'What a damnable villain!' said Bowlemover, glaring through his spectacles at the astonished prisoner—'a damnable villain! String him up, Mastodon; string him up.'

'Do you acknowledge the authorship of this last production?' continued Sir Mastodon, addressing the prisoner, and not deigning to notice his colleague's remark.

'Most certainly not,' replied Thurston indignantly. 'I have nothing to say to it, and my signature at the foot must be a forgery.'

'Now,' said Sir Marmaduke, turning to to Bowlemover and speaking at the prisoner, 'you observe he denies the authorship of the last proclamation, though he admits that of the former ones. The signature is precisely the same in all. These proclamations were printed off to the number of ten thousand in one day, and circulated not only throughout the city of Delhi, but throughout Hindoostan. You may judge of the effect they had.'

'A damnable villain!' repeated Bowlemover *sotto voce*, still glaring through his spectacles.

'The emissary alluded to in the last document,' continued Sir Marmaduke mercilessly, 'is thus described by my spy. The descriptive roll I will now read out, and you can judge, Bowlemover, if it applies to the prisoner or not:

'"Height, five feet ten and a half; nose, aquiline; eyes, blue; hair, reddish-brown; age, about thirty-nine or forty; scar over the left eye."'

'Upon my soul it is a life-like portrait,' said Bowlemover.

'Have you any objection to bare your right shoulder?' asked Sir Marmaduke. 'The descriptive roll alludes to a scar of an old wound upon the right shoulder, between that and the neck.'

'It may save trouble,' replied Thurston, 'if I acknowledge I have a scar in that very place, the effect of an accident with a gun that occurred when I was a boy.'

'Have you anything to urge in your defence?' said Sir Marmaduke, throwing the roll of papers he held in his hand carelessly on the table, putting his hands in his pockets, and leaning back in his chair.

It will not be necessary for me to detail the prisoner's defence. He seemed at last thoroughly awakened to the serious nature of his position and of the charge made against him, and applied himself to his defence right vigorously. He insisted that he was not to blame for treasonable proclamations being issued in his name; even though the substance of some of those proclamations had actually been the product of his pen, they were never intended for the use they had been put to. He asserted his right as a British subject to be tried by a jury of his peers, declared the whole proceedings arbitrary and illegal, and denied the authority of the judges who sat before him, judges *de facto*, but not *de jure* to interfere with his liberty as a British subject at all, and finally wound up by threatening them both with the severe displeasure of the House of Commons and the British public.

Sir Marmaduke and Bowlemover held a short consultation together in an undertone after Thurston had concluded his defence, when the former, having received an intimation of assent from his colleague, proceeded to address the prisoner in a very serious tone. He said both he and his learned colleague had come to the unanimous conclusion that the prisoner was clearly proved guilty of aiding, abetting, and instigating rebellion and murder. That no doubt existed in their minds that he was the emissary alluded to in the proclamation, and therefore not a British subject. The prisoner had not chosen to avail himself of his right to call any witnesses, the reason of which he fully understood, viz. that the only two witnesses of importance he could call, Mr. Dacres and Captain Murray, were prepared to convict him on their joint evidence of a foul and detestable murder. The prisoner had passed himself off as an Englishman; but Sir Marmaduke was happy to think he was spared the pain of inflicting punishment on one of his own countrymen—pain that would be aggravated a thousand-fold by the reflection that any Englishman could so thoroughly disgrace his national character as to give utterance to sentiments like those publicly promulgated by the prisoner, for which he would now suffer deservedly, whether Englishman or not, the severest penalty of the law. He concluded by informing him that he was sentenced to death, and would be hanged the next morning at sunrise. 'The prisoner,' he added, 'had objected to informality of procedure, but he might set himself at rest on that score, as all such proceedings in India were kept on record, and a full report of the trial and execution would be forwarded hereafter to the Supreme Government for their information and approval.'

He then turned to an orderly and directed him to summon the provost sergeant. That functionary was in attendance almost before the now astounded prisoner had recovered his breath, which had been fairly driven out of his body by the forcible and very personal remarks he had just listened to. He was as pale as ashes.

'Sergeant Windpipe, this is your prisoner: you will take him away, put him in confinement, and see that he is hanged to-morrow at sunrise.'

Sergeant Windpipe made a military salute, and said,

'Yes, sir.'

Mr. Thurston again essayed to stammer forth some protest against the sentence. At a sign from Sir Marmaduke, however, Serjeant Windpipe, aided by the Sikh guard, collared and led him out.

'Now let's to dinner,' said Sir Marmaduke to Bowlemover as soon as they were alone. 'That fellow has kept us longer than I expected.'

'A damnable villain,' repeated Bowlemover *sotto voce*, as he walked into the other tent where dinner awaited them—'a most damnable villain.'

Dacres read carefully the papers Sir Marmaduke had given him all through, English and Persian, without once looking up or speaking a word. When he had finished, he raised his head and said,

'Where did you get hold of these, Sir Marmaduke?'

'My spy brought them to me.'

'Have you confronted the spy with the accused? for it seems to me that he is the real prosecutor and witness in this case.'

'No, I did not think it necessary,' said Sir Marmaduke, rather curtly, 'and the prisoner did not call for it.'

'Have you any objection to confronting him with me now?'

'None, if you particularly wish it, though I hardly know how it is to be managed, for he has been very ill ever since I left Aurungabad for this place, and forced to travel in a litter.'

'Here is Dr. Mactartan coming,' said Dacres; 'he will doubtless see the spy, and tell us if he is fit to be moved.'

Mactartan rode up, attracted by curiosity to see what the little knot of persons were doing there under the tree, just as Dacres had done speaking, and, at that gentleman's request, immediately consented to accompany Sir Marmaduke's mounted orderly to the camp of the important personage who held the office of Sir Marmaduke's chief informer, spy, and head of the intelligence department.

After a very awkward silence of about ten minutes, during which Dacres occupied himself with re-examining the papers he held in his hand, while Sir Marmaduke smoked a cheroot, and Thurston, released for a time from the vilest of all vile durance, that of a halter round one's neck, sat on the ground under the tree which was so nearly becoming his gallows, and meditated, as it is to be hoped profitably, on the vicissitudes of human life—after about ten minutes passed in this way, Dr. Mactartan cantered up, saying he had examined Syud Abdul Hussan (for such was the spy's name), and found him, though weak, quite able to come so far as that in a palanquin, and stating moreover that he was on his way.

After some further delay, the palanquin bearing the Syud, accompanied by several runners, and Sir Marmaduke's orderly bringing up the rear, approached. On the palanquin being set down, and the occupant being desired to come out, the greatest difficulty was experienced in attaining this result. He steadily and absolutely refused to listen to any request, entreaty, or command. He had come thus far, indeed, under the stringent order given by the mounted orderly and confirmed by Dr. Mactartan's visit, but get out of the palanquin or show himself he would not. His opposition to so simple a request aroused Dacres' suspicions, and he desired Dr. Mactartan again to examine and report whether there was anything in the present state of his health to justify his obstinate refusal to undergo the exertion of getting out of the palanquin. Dr. Mactartan again examined the patient, and declared his belief that he was shamming. Sir Marmaduke was not a man to stand this even from a favourite, so he intimated to the Syud Abdul Hussan that if he did not forthwith present himself as ordered, he would be dragged out of his retirement by force by the Sikh orderlies. Thus urged by a voice whose tone of command he at once unwillingly recognised, Syud Abdul Hussan turned unwillingly and reluctantly enough out of his palanquin, and presented himself to the assembled group.

Dacres, as soon as he set eyes on the Syud, laughed outright. The effect of his appearance on Thurston was most marvellous. That gentleman, although his arms were still pinioned, had his legs free. The instant Syud Abdul Hussan appeared, he jumped up with a yell in which hatred, joy, triumph, despair, and hope were strangely intermingled, and commenced dancing about as if he was a maniac escaped from Bedlam; the efforts necessary to effect this saltatory exercise with his arms pinioned close to his sides, as is the manner with men who are about to be hanged, affording a most grotesquely horrible spectacle.

Sir Marmaduke looked on amazed. Dacres was the first to break silence; he ejaculated,

'Wily Mahomed! by Jove!'

It will not be necessary for me to lengthen this narrative by detailing the explanation that followed the declaration of the true character of Syud Abdul Hussan, which the reader will easily understand. All was plain now. Wily Mahomed had possessed himself of all Thurston's private papers, and made good use of them, playing first into the hands of the rebels whom he easily deceived by counterfeit seals and signatures, and then into the hands of the English authorities.

The explanation and examination ended in Thurston's being released, and Wily Mahomed's neck being placed in the noose instead of his.

He prepared to meet his fate with stoical apathy. All the spectators of this awful scene, used as they had been of late to witness death in all its forms, preserved a solemn silence suited to the occasion. Just before the last act of the tragedy was perpetrated by Sergeant Windpipe, and as the unhappy Wily Mahomed stood on the edge of the cart which was to him indeed the brink of eternity, Thurston suddenly jumped forward, made a kind of triumphal Indian war-dance in front of the condemned, and concluded by spitting in his face. This was the last act of grace Wily Mahomed received from man; the next moment his body was dangling between air and earth, and his soul was struggling to free itself from its mortal tenement.

Thurston's barbarous behaviour called forth a murmur of disgust from all the officers present. Dacres could not contain himself. As the rest rode slowly away, he turned and said,

'You mean, base, cowardly cur, with less feeling than a dog, more mean ten thousand times than the unhappy wretch you have insulted at the moment when human justice had nothing further to claim from him—go and blazon forth your hypocrisy before the world, and blister your tongue with fresh lies and scandals against your fellow-countrymen. Recollect Asgar Ally—a finer fellow never breathed. You have escaped being hanged this time, but if ever a murderer with his hands stained with innocent blood deserved hanging, you do.'

'By Jove, I forgot about that,' said Sir Marmaduke, checking his horse as he was riding off with Dacres. 'I forgot that nice little story about Asgar Ally.'

'No, no, Sir Marmaduke,' said Dacres, 'let him go, the mean-spirited cur that he is: our blood was heated at the time, and we were so used to see it flow that we forgot its value in the eyes of God, and the penalty for rashly taking human life. It was a murder—a foul murder; but let us leave him to his own conscience and his Maker.'

'His conscience! faith, that will trouble him but little. Suppose we give him a few dozen —it will be a lesson to him.'

'Lessons he has had and plenty, and I trust will profit by them. No, Sir Marmaduke, let him go. I don't like to see my fellow-countrymen degraded—though it is degradation enough to have to call oneself a fellow-countryman of his. I vowed a solemn vow that he should be called on to answer for the crime of murder, as I stood by the side of Asgar Ally's bleeding corpse. But let that pass; such vows are more honoured in their breach than their observance. We won't sully our victory by the execution of one of our own countrymen who has run the gauntlet with us, much as he deserves it.'

Sir Marmaduke yielded, though with reluctance, to the persuasion of his companion, and they rode away together. Thurston went off in another direction. Dacres thought he had had the last of him, but was mistaken, as will appear anon.

CHAPTER LVIII.

Late that evening Dacres, who, fairly worn out with exhaustion, had thrown himself upon his bed early in the afternoon, and sunk into a deep sleep, was startled from his slumbers by some one calling to him impatiently and loudly from outside the tent.

'Dacres! Dacres! are you in?'

'Yes, what's up?' he cried. 'Ah, is it you, Graham? come in.'

'I've got him,' said Graham.

'Got him—who?'

'I went out scouring the country with some of these Sikhs—splendid fellows they are—and I found him lying half dead, like a dog in a ditch, and I've brought him on a litter. There's a little breath left in him yet; let's give him some brandy, and see if we can dress his wounds. He will be able to tell us a lot that we want to know.'

'What's it all about?' said Dacres, only half awake.

'The Mirza! I've caught the Mirza!' said

Graham, entering the tent. 'There wasn't much catching in it, though, for I found him in a ditch; here a lot of Sikhs have brought him in on a litter on their heads—see, here he comes.'

As he spoke four Sikhs came up to the tent door with a litter, which they deposited on the ground. Dacres, at length aroused, brought a light, and they examined the dying man together. He was a frightful spectacle. His clothes had been saturated with blood, which had dried upon them, and they were now clotted and stiff, and he was covered with dirt and mud. So badly wounded as to be unable to make good his escape, though supported by his own innate energy and spirit to the last, he had ridden as long as he had strength to sit his horse. In doing this he had taxed his physical powers to the utmost, and when they gave way he was forced to lie, helpless and unbefriended, at the bottom of the ditch he fell into. Here Graham found him.

The attempt to remove the wounded man's clothes occasioned him such agony that they abandoned it after the first trial. The wounds appeared to be mortal, and after a short consultation they determined to send for Dr. Mactartan.

'Spare yourselves the trouble of sending

for medical assistance,' said the dying man, in a faint voice, and in good English.

Dacres and Graham started, and looked at one another—a ghastly imitation of a smile passed across the haggard features of the Mirza.

'You speak English, then?' said Dacres, addressing him; 'is it true that you are indeed what I have heard, one of our own countrymen—a renegade—a traitor to your country—and your God?' he added, after a pause, as if he wished to say it, but was unwilling to appear guilty of taunting the traitor on his death-bed.

'Call me what you will—hard words break no bones—and it would matter little if they did—to me now. I am one who has made shipwreck of life—missed the prize when it was all but within my reach. Regrets are vain—leave me to die in peace; or, if you want to make a sacrifice to justice, and to trample out with violence the few sparks of life that still linger in me, do so at once. My wounds are mortal, no art can heal them—kill me or leave me, it's all one.'

'Your life is justly forfeited to the outraged laws of your country,' said Dacres; 'but if it is as you say, we can safely leave you to plead your own cause before that tribunal at which you must soon appear. Yet you may make a last atonement for a life of crime by giving us all the information you can respecting the plans and prospects of the rebels and murderers you have lately been associated with. From man you have no mercy to expect, even if you survive these wounds, but with God the fountain of mercy is ever flowing. Tell me, are you or were you baptized in the Christian faith?'

A pang of mortal agony seemed to shoot through the frame of the dying man; it might be from the rapid internal inflammation from his wounds, or it might be from some deep emotion stirred up by the simple question just asked him. He closed his eyes, and compressed his livid lips together as if in extreme suffering. It was some little time before he was able to speak; when he opened his mouth he articulated his words with difficulty, and his breath came short and thick.

'I will tell you who I was, if I have time, and will tell you something more. You are right in one thing; I am, at least I was—an Englishman.'

'God have mercy on you,' said Graham, with a loathing he could not suppress for the man who had betrayed his country and his faith.

'Give us what information you can about the rebels and their plot; it is the only reparation you can make,' said Dacres.

'Reparation! ah, you would have me add to all my other crimes that of double treachery and perjury at the last moment?'

'An oath that it is sin to make, it is sin to keep.'

'There are some things on my conscience I would first get rid of,' said the dying man, after a long pause, during which he remained wrapt in thought, and then continued—'I left home when I was young; I served in the Russian army in the Caucasus, was taken prisoner there, and changed my faith to save my wretched life. Naturalised as a Circassian, I fought in five campaigns against the invader. I had a wife there, and a happy home and two children. Home! ah, but it is a long story, and I am growing faint. What if there is a future, after all?'

They plied him with brandy and restoratives, and, by degrees, collected from his lips, in broken sentences and incoherent language, the following facts about his life, which I will give in a collected form.

'I fled or was driven out of Circassia for reasons I need not detail, and thence wandered into Persia. I was useful at the Persian Court, where I got recommended by a nobleman whose service I entered as an armed retainer. I had embraced the Mahometan religion long before this. My genius, great naturally, had been fostered by instruction. I had received a medical education in England before I ran away from home, and, first to gratify a whim, and afterwards with a serious design to advance my fortunes in life by such means, I studied and mastered all the tricks and arts by which professional conjurors get their living. Mesmerism I practised most successfully. I could pick up any language of any people among whom I lived in six months, and by one means and another speedily acquired reputation, and with it wealth; with this came ambition. For a long time I laboured to carry out a scheme I entertained of founding a sovereignty in Central Asia; but circumstance, in which I always placed blind confidence, brought me to Cabul, and thence to India. Here there was a golden harvest awaiting me; gold and silver—aye, more, honour, dignity, influence, were all to be picked up in the high roads. I soon perceived what was going on, and that the country was ripe for revolt; and I saw the opening there was for me. By means of trickery, and apparatus always at hand, and my natural talent for imposing on others, I soon made the superstitious and excitable natives look on me as a prophet. From that moment I was safe. Once my religious character and my divine mission was believed in, and I could do anything I liked. If I failed, the failure cost me nothing; I could explain it away. Riches poured into my lap; I spent freely the money I freely received, and so my influence became unbounded. I mixed with Europeans, and heard all that they said about the natives; and I mixed with natives, and heard all that they had to say about Europeans. The golden apples dropt into my hand; I had but to stretch it out to take them. The wealth I amassed was enormous. Success never failed me in any of my schemes or projects; I stepped from one position of advantage to another, and beheld all that was rich and worth having in India at my feet. If this rebellion, well planned, had been well carried out, as I and others intended it should be, my position would have been a dazzling one. There was but one path to it, though, and that was through blood, and where there is strife there are blows dealt on both sides. At last the tide turned, but only yesterday; and here I am, ruined—aye, worse than ruined.'

'And the plot? tell us more of the plot,' asked Dacres eagerly. 'Who has been at the bottom of it? Is there more than we see on the surface, or is it merely a sudden outbreak of military discontent?'

The dying man shook his head, as if unable to speak; life was ebbing fast, but the near approach of death seemed to awaken a feeling in his heart akin to remorse. He opened his eyes, and staring wildly at Graham, caught his hand with a convulsive grasp.

'Give me one promise,' he said; 'you look as if I could trust you—though I never trusted mortal yet. Will you swear?'

'What is it? I will do anything that is reasonable, and anything that is just and honourable, but I will swear no oath in the dark.'

'It is this,' said the dying man; 'I will tell you where all that remains of my wealth is to be found—take it to—my poor old father, if he yet lives—and tell him it was the last parting gift from his ungrateful son, and that at my last moment I thought of him.'

'But about the mutiny?' said Dacres, 'tell us who planned it, who set it on foot?'

'I will, I will, I know it all—all; but first swear.'

'No, I will swear nothing,' said Graham, 'but I will, if you wish it, and if I can find it, take all your ill-gotten wealth to England; and your father, who is he? where and how shall I find him? where does he live?'

'His name is Graham—he was in the Indian army—he left it as a colonel.'

The blood left Graham's cheek, he became white as ashes, and bending down over the prostrate form before him, he whispered in his ear,

'Had you any brother and sister?—and your mother?'

'She died in the Cabul war. I had one brother—I never saw my sister.'

'Harry!' again whispered Graham, pressing the clammy hand he held within his own.

The Mirza turned his eyes upon the speaker, and gazed into them with a look Graham never forgot till his dying day. There was no further doubt about the matter; he had sunk on one knee, and was supporting the head of the dying man upon his lap. It was his own brother whose last agonies he was watching.

It is needless to say that Dacres was intensely interested in the scene. He could do little but watch, for the two had become so absorbed in the astounding truth laid bare to them, that they appeared unconscious of the presence even of a third person. He was, however, terribly anxious to get some more information out of the renegade before he breathed his last, which it was evident he could give; but it became more doubtful every moment whether his rapidly failing strength would allow him to speak. In broken accents, and in a whisper, he gave his brother the necessary directions by which he could find his residence, which was in an independent state in Central India, and where the whole of his hoarded wealth was concealed. In broken accents, too, he imparted his last wishes respecting the female inmates of his palace who had shared his hours of luxurious indolence and pandered to his passions. By dint of questions put to him, and answered partly by monosyllables and sometimes by signs, Graham, at Dacres' dictation, elicited a few facts from him.

'The mutiny had been preparing for many years; it was not the growth of a moment, not a passing impulse, but the result of feelings that had long been in existence throughout the native army, and long gaining strength. Undoubtedly Mahometan influence was the moving spring of it all, and the superstitions of the Hindoos were made by them a tool for working out the end—the destruction of the British empire.

'By a strange concatenation of fortuitous circumstances had these schemes and plots been fostered. The Cabul massacre first opened the eyes of the sepoys and of the disaffected natives to what might be done by combination. The feeling grew and gained strength year by year. The Russian war and the reported and commonly believed defeat of the English and French by the Russians, and above all, the fall of Kars, which was magnified into an event of the first importance, all added fuel to the flame that was now smouldering. The leading conspirators, chief men in all the largest and wealthiest cities in India, had for long been in correspondence. The disaffection was spread all over Upper and a great part of Lower India, like a network: the cleverest men were selected for agents and emissaries. Yet these were only trusted so far as to enable them to do the errands they were sent upon, and only to such an extent, that if disposed to turn traitors, they could do no harm, for they had nothing tangible, nothing certain to reveal. The Delhi Court was the focus of the insurrection, the centre from whence all the springs of the great plot emanated, to which all eyes, all hopes were turned. The whole native mind was kept excited, mystified, aroused, suspicious. No stone was left unturned, no means untried, to foster this feeling of unquiet and restlessness; so that every man and woman was on the look-out for something striking and wonderful that was to occur, no one exactly knew what or when. This had been the state of things for a long while: a feeling gathering intensity as time went on and suspense was prolonged. It was a covered magazine, and the train was laid: all that was wanted was the spark, and that the British Government applied themselves, by the cartridges.

'So skilfully was every engine worked, every motive appealed to, that no class were excluded. The restless and disaffected part of the population were excited by wild hopes of an approaching period of anarchy, in which they would make a rich harvest. The ambitious and intriguing men saw in the coming crisis a field for the display of their powers, a tangible object for their ambition to strain at. The wealthy classes, who might be supposed averse to violent political changes, as having everything to lose and nothing to gain, were worked upon by fear for their religion, which, it was pointed out to them, was in danger from the persevering efforts of Christian missionaries, and the zeal with which the Government pressed on their scheme for education. The independent princes, so far as they were trusted with the design of the conspirators, were bid to remain aloof as long as it was their policy to do so, or bribed to a negative partisanship by vague hopes of extended influence and power. Some, who were not to be trusted at all, were kept completely in the dark, or their suspicions, if aroused, easily allayed. So widely were the ramifications of this plot extended, that even the few who were resolved to abide by their allegiance through good or ill, were at times staggered in their belief in the power of the British Government. It was difficult, nay, impossible for them to obtain accurate knowledge of the state of Europe, or of passing and recent events. They were told that England was so weakened by the Russian war that she had no troops to send; they looked around, and beheld a striking confirmation of the rumour in the scanty garrisons of English soldiers that remained in India. The treasuries, the arsenals, the strongholds of the country, were all in the hands of the native soldiers. The English themselves a mere handful in the country; while the Mahometan powers of Central Asia were ready to swoop down upon the plains of Hindustan, to aid the struggle for the faith of Islam. The difficulties England would have to encounter in case of a rebellion, set forth and dwelt upon by English writers themselves, were represented, exaggerated, repeated; while dreams, portents, omens, and prophecies were multiplied and reiterated, to keep the superstitious feelings of the whole mass of the people, educated and uneducated, for they were all alike amenable to impulses of this nature, in a state of constant agitation; and all these engines were worked incessantly through the native press, over which there were neither censorship nor supervision exercised, except by those behind the scenes.'

All this was communicated, as I said before, by the dying man by means of signs and monosyllabic answers to questions. It took a long time to worm it out of him, and once or twice Dacres and Graham thought his spirit had fled. The event came at last; he ceased to speak, or to show any signs of vitality at all; he still breathed, but his breath came and went with difficulty, and occasionally there was so long a hiatus that they thought all was over. He was not destined, however, to pass so quietly from the world; the flame burnt up again and flickered convulsively ere it went out, and his last moments were spent in a terrible struggle with death, and in a state of mortal anguish which it was most painful to behold. The soul, burdened with the load of crime the blackest and the most deadly that the human heart in open rebellion against its Creator can be guilty of, clung with agonised fear and convulsive trembling to its tenement of clay. But death had laid its inexorable hand upon him, and with a suppressed cry of agony that rang in the ears of those who heard it for many a long year afterwards, the soul of the renegade passed unshriven into the presence of its Maker.

CHAPTER LIX.

The wild cry that rang above the din of battle, as Amy fell senseless on her lover's breast, was the last sound that was to proceed from those pale lips for many a weary month. The unparalleled efforts which had buoyed her up through every kind of hardship and misery, had at last told on her intellectual and physical organisation, and it seemed for a time as if both had been crushed by the burden. In the moment of relief and joy, when weaker ones were forgetting their sorrows and predicting a happier future, the brightest, loveliest, and best was alone overcome; and the youthful fire which had shed light on the darkest places was now a flickering spark, which a mere breath of wind might extinguish. Throughout the whole of their trials the actual pressure upon Amy had been greater than that experienced by any of her female companions. Strange as it may seem, she, without family ties, had more strain on her mind than the married ladies who had half-a-dozen children to attend to. A little reflection will explain this. The latter were allowed, as was reasonable, to attend to their respective families exclusively, such being the function that nature pointed out as peculiarly their own; while Amy had no such special avocation, and was therefore at everybody's beck and call. She did her duty nobly, and spared neither bodily nor mental exertion. Whether a soldier wanted ammunition, a sick lady wanted attendance, or a baby wanted food, it was all one; Amy was the person to get it, and everybody at last seemed to rely upon her for everything, as if she had had all the resources of the world at her command. But this was not all: it was felt very soon that she was worthy to take a part in the general consultations; and her practical suggestions were often found useful when military science was puzzled by the anomalies of barbarous warfare, or when Dacres the civilian grew warm in debate with Murray the 'irregular.' It was singular and touching to behold a young and high-bred lady sitting in council with the powder-stained heroes of the fight, and to see bearded warriors pondering gravely over her remarks, or answering her shortly and sharply, as if talking to one of their own sex and profession. Yet this and everything else seemed natural after a little while, and it was only in an occasional day-dream that the strange reality seemed indeed to be strange. Then, for a moment, our friends would wonder at their own obtuseness, and would ask themselves in their secret hearts whether an angel had been sent to comfort and encourage them in their dire distress.

Perhaps even the extreme tension to which Amy was subjected would have failed to injure her in health or mind, if she had not been struck down suddenly by the tidings of Graham's supposed decease. She could not doubt the truth of the intelligence, and, believing it, she felt as if all her impulse to exertion was gone. It followed from this that every effort was against the grain. To a careless observer, indeed, there was little difference, for she now did the same things from motives of duty which had been a labour of love before. When she hoped to see Graham march triumphantly to the relief of the garrison, she cared little for fatigue, and less for danger. Such was her confidence in her lover, that the happy end was ever before her, and the hardships of the intermediate time seemed scarcely worth a thought. But now everything was changed: the glorious picture in the distance was gone, and the bare foreground was visible in all its hopeless sterility. When she suddenly saw Graham in the midst of the fight, the shock was too violent, and the mind was incapable of bearing the reaction. The buoyancy of the vessel was gone—the bark refused to rise to the wave, and the sea that should have borne it into port had well-nigh engulphed it for ever.

It is needless to say that Amy received during her illness all the attention that the most heartfelt gratitude and affection could suggest. All who had been imprisoned in the tomb justly looked upon Graham as their deliverer; and that was an additional reason, if any had been required, for bestowing all their care upon the girl he loved. In time, the fever reached a climax, and for a few hours Amy hovered between life and death. It would be impossible to describe Graham's feelings at this crisis, or his joy when good Dr. Mactartan rushed in upon him and wrung his hand, assuring him, more by gesture than by words (for the rough but warm-hearted doctor himself was almost speechless with emotion), that all immediate danger was over. By degrees Amy gained strength, and was said in medical parlance to be 'going on well;' but almost as soon as the first fear—the fear of death—was past, another scarcely less terrible apprehension arose. It was found that she had a very imperfect recollection of the events of the last few months, and it was feared that her mind had suffered an irremediable injury. Little by little, it is true, she was able to converse about some of the circumstances; but it was only by fits and starts, and she seemed unable to connect the whole story. The death of Burleigh and the re-appearance of Graham had been witnessed by her in the last moment of consciousness, and apparently the mind had not had time to comprehend what had been presented to the eye. Over and over again her friends endeavoured to explain how matters stood, but she could only understand one thing at a time. If they assured her that Graham lived, she remembered her hateful engagement to Burleigh; and when she was told that Burleigh's death had set her free, she believed that Graham was lying unburied in the sultry desert. Thus she knew not whither to turn for comfort, and she gave way to a settled melancholy which filled her friends with the most painful apprehensions.

It was thought best to remove her from the scene of her trials; and she was brought to Europe, and went to stay with some relations on the south-west coast of England. Here, in peace and repose, far from everything that could remind her of the past, there was the best chance of her recovering from the inexplicable lethargy which oppressed her. At first they began to have good hopes of her amendment, as the novelty of the scene seemed to excite her, and she took pleasure in sitting on the sunny cliffs and watching the ever-changing face of the ocean. But these happy auguries were of short duration, for no decided change took place, and the mind remained like a smooth lake, glistening sometimes in the sunshine, but never flowing like the waters of a living stream.

In the meantime Graham came home from India, all unconscious of the sad news that awaited him. He had not been allowed to see Amy during her convalescence, as it was feared that the surprise might be too much for her in her weak state, and might cause a relapse. Judge of his agony when, on reaching his native shore, he was still forbidden to approach her, and was told in gentle but unmistakeable language that he must not expect to find her what she had been before! His career had been prosperous, his worldly prospects were even brilliant; but what was the use of wealth and position now? All his hope in life was gone, all his happy castle-building was dashed to the ground. He wrung his hands in anguish, and wished that he was lying by the side of poor Harley in the desert.

What to do next he knew not. He had been forming all sorts of plans on the voyage home, but all those plans were in some manner connected with one object—that of making Amy a happy wife. Now it seemed to him that there was no result in life to be gained, that it mattered little what his actions were, and that all he could do was to vegetate from day to day. After a time this morbid feeling began to affect his health, and some of his friends, alarmed at the symptoms displayed in his present appearance, strongly advised him to try a change of scene. He acquiesced, in a quiet, listless manner, but secretly determined that his excursion should be so arranged as to bring him, if only for a moment, near the place where Amy was living. Accordingly, he started from the metropolis in a south-westerly direction, and a few hours' journey brought him to a little town in Hampshire, from which he speedily passed into the neighbouring county of Dorset. From this point he started alone on a walking tour, which was to extend round the whole English coast; but his solitary journey was brought to a termination rather sooner than he expected.

There is no doubt that to the weak mind of

man, mere change is a great regenerator. It prevents us from dwelling incessantly on our grievances and misfortunes, and gives us time to recruit, just as an occasional rest gives us fresh courage to push on in a weary journey. As Graham walked along the towering cliffs and descended into the hollow bottoms of the Isle of Purbeck, he now and then during a brief interval forgot his woes in contemplating the glories of that magnificent coast. The fresh sea-breeze seemed like a cordial, and he was sometimes almost angry with himself for feeling for a moment as if the great scheme of nature included other beings beside himself and Amy. One afternoon he crossed the ridge which forms the western boundary of Purbeck, and towards evening he found himself, after one or two rather rash descents, in a spot more beautiful than any that he had yet seen or imagined. He stood on a kind of small inland cliff which rose outwards till it towered proudly over the open sea. On the right and in front were various forms of rock and down, some rising with a broad sweep, others presenting the strata boldly to the air. At his feet lay a miniature piece of the ocean, with a microscopic beach of its own, and a single channel between two picturesque headlands to connect it with the sea without. A crystal stream gushed from the base of the hills, formed a mimic lake, turned a mill, and, after living for an hour like the May-fly, lost itself amid the pebbles of the shore. The sun can glorify even mean scenery; and he was now blazing in full splendour, and doing his best to make Lulworth Cove a scene of enchantment.

Graham had never been insensible to the beauties of nature, and, in spite of his depressed state, he stood motionless in admiration. He might have remained spell-bound for a long time, had he not been suddenly made aware that he was not alone. The rustle of a silken dress startled him from his reverie, and on looking round he saw a lady, whom his presence had apparently disturbed, and who was rising from a knoll behind which she had sat concealed. In turning round, she looked unavoidably towards him, and their eyes met. He hesitated, but only for a moment, and then he wildly cried 'Amy!' and Amy rushed into his arms.

It was long before either of them had sufficient calmness to enter into explanations. Indeed, he feared at first that he had found Amy only to lose her again, for after the first impulse of feeling she fainted away, and seemed as one dead. When she recovered, she sat by him, and appeared, although still trembling and afraid to look up, to derive courage and comfort from feeling his arm around her.

They sat for a long time in silence, but at length Amy looked up timidly and said,

'But is it you really, Arthur?' They told me you were ——'

She could not bear to finish the sentence; but Graham understood her, and pressed her more closely to him. She was reassured by this material proof of his existence, and listened calmly, though evidently a little puzzled, while he told her how the mistake had arisen, and how that he was really her own Arthur, and had come to explain the truth to her. Happy man! he could rely on his own strength now, for he felt instinctively that his presence had effected a cure. They were both silent again for many minutes; and then Amy put her hand to her forehead, and said,

'I have been trying to recollect, and I think I understand it all now; but will you tell me once more?'

He told her the glad news again and again, and each time she understood it better than before. When she trembled, as she did still from time to time, he had only to fold his arm more closely around her, and she believed and was strong again. The little waves of Lulworth Cove danced up in the sunshine, and seemed to rejoice with the lovers; and many years afterwards, they remembered the tiny billows, though then they knew not that they heeded them. The sun went down, and the wavelets danced in the twilight, and still they sat and thought, but spoke little. When they moved away at last, the shades of night obscured the landscape; but it mattered little to Amy and Arthur, for the sun of love was in their hearts.

CHAPTER LX.

All that I have now left to do, is to gather together the scattered threads of my story and wind them up.

As soon as the roads were safe for travelling, Mr. Thurston repaired to Calcutta, *en route* for England. The Governor-General hearing accidentally that there was a gentleman in Calcutta recently arrived from the disturbed provinces, who, while travelling in India, had been drawn into the vortex of the rebellion, and had been a witness, albeit an unwilling one, of all that went on, sent for him. Mr. Thurston was closeted for upwards of an hour with the Governor-General, and, no doubt, communicated freely to that functionary his views of public matters and recent occurrences. The next day, the following letter was despatched to Mr. Dacres:—

'*From the Secretary to the Governor-General in Council, to Mr. Dacres, C.S., Commissioner of Islamabad, Central Provinces.*

'FORT WILLIAM: *August* —, 1857.

'SIR,—His Excellency in Council desires me to inform you that he has heard with much regret, from independent testimony which it is impossible to doubt, many circumstances which substantiate various reports His Excellency has already received regarding certain unconstitutional and illegal measures adopted by you during the recent disturbances. Although His Excellency in Council is fully prepared to make every allowance for the difficulties which beset almost all the executive civil officers of government in the disaffected districts during the recent disturbances, and would not hesitate to sanction a reasonable departure, under circumstances of such emergency, from the rules and regulations laid down for the guidance of executive officers in ordinary times; yet His Excellency in Council regrets that you should have allowed yourself to be so carried away by a temporary, and what would have been, but for the injudicious behaviour of public officers, but a groundless panic, as to inaugurate, sanction, and carry out violent and unconstitutional measures, which there was nothing in reality to justify.

'The main points in which your recent conduct of public affairs has more particularly met with the disapproval of His Excellency in Council are the following:—

'1. In sending for military aid and suggesting the movements of troops without reference to the head of the government.

'2. In creating a mischievous panic in the district by unnecessary collection of supplies for troops.

'3. In withdrawing the native troops from the military cantonment of Islamabad without the orders of government.

'4. In needlessly exposing officers to the inclemency of the weather and danger from the rebels, by deputing the late Mr. Harley and Lieutenant Graham from Islamabad to Aurungabad.

'5. In holding communication and connecting yourself with the Nawab of Islamabad, who is proved by ample testimony to have been one of the foremost among the ringleaders of the late disturbances.

'6. In compromising the British government, by repairing with the European residents of Islamabad to the Nawab's palace and taking up your abode there.

'7. In the wanton destruction of Ali Moorad's house, for which a claim for compensation has been sent in.

'8. In needlessly outraging the feelings of the natives, by occupying as a residence the sacred tomb of Chunder Bagh.

'Before passing any final order on the question, His Excellency in Council will be glad to hear any explanation you may wish to offer on the above points.

'I have the honour to be, Sir,

'Your most obedient servant,

'JAMES CURFEW BELL,

'Secretary to Government.'

Dacres was not an ambitious man. Wearied out by a long term of service, during which he had been unremitting in his attention to his public duties, and with his constitution a good deal shattered by the exposure and excitement and hardships he had recently gone through, he had begun to look forward to an early and honourable retirement from the service. Conscious, however, that, under Providence, the survivors of the terrible catastrophe at Islamabad owed their lives to him, and that the government no less owed the preservation of the whole district to his energy, he could not be so blind to his own merits as not to feel pained at the receipt of the above letter. He was entitled to his pension; and feeling sure that all his fellow-countrymen who were cognisant of the real state of affairs would give him the credit which his superiors, under the influence of interested and designing persons, refused him, and buoyed up by the conviction that history, if she ever descended to the details of the great rebellion, would do him, and others like him, ample justice, he did not allow the matter to weigh upon his spirits. In reply to the letter, however, he forwarded a detailed report of everything that had taken place at Islamabad since the beginning of the outbreak, when communication with the outside world had been cut off. What gave him much more concern than any allusion to his own conduct in the affair was the statement regarding the Nawab, who, it was evident, had fallen, like himself, a victim to intrigue or ignorance. In his report he was far more careful to put down every circumstance that might serve to place in a proper and true light the eminent services of the Nawab than to justify or defend himself. Unhappily, it was of no avail. The following order in the

'Government Gazette' was the only reply that was vouchsafed to his letter:—

'No. 18,675,096.

'FORT WILLIAM: *August* 31, 1857.

'The Governor-General in Council has been pleased to appoint Quintilian Edward Dormouse, C.S., to be Commissioner of Islamabad. Mr. Dormouse is directed to proceed at once to Islamabad and receive charge of the district from Mr. Dacres, C.S.'

By the usages of the service, this order constructively forced Mr. Dacres to retire upon his pension.

The Nawab's estates were at the same time confiscated. Dacres endeavoured to console him under this fresh stroke of adverse fate, and promised to intercede with the superior authorities in England, and get him reinstated. All in vain. He sickened and took to his bed. Dacres would not leave him, though all his preparations were made and there was nothing to detain him in the country, and he was anxious to return to England to his wife and children. He was not detained long. Two days after the arrival of the fatal order, the Nawab died of a broken heart, but not before he had given into Dacres's hand the letter he wrote and caused to be signed by two of his ministers, on the day that he took the field under compulsion at the head of the troops, which proved incontestably his innocence.

As the government at the restoration of peace deemed it very desirable to place some of the long-neglected members of the old aristocracy of India in the position of wealthy landholders, by conferring upon them estates which had been confiscated for the rebellion of their owners, an old table servant of Mr. Dormouse, named Peer Bux, having persuaded that gentleman that he was one of the oldest families in the country, was recommended as a worthy recipient of the estates, honours, and titles of the Nawab of Islamabad, and shortly after installed therein by orders of government.

I cannot say how long Amy and Graham remained on the cliff that evening at Lulworth Cove, for they never told me. Indeed, I do not think they knew much about it themselves; and Graham was certainly heard to assert that his watch had stopped the day before, and that he had lost all count of time. To the disgrace of human nature, I regret to say that nobody could be found to believe him; but it is certain (and this is more to the point) that from that moment Amy's illusions very seldom recurred, and that Graham's presence never failed to dispel them immediately. I recommend the case particularly to the attention of my medical friends, and especially to those who take an interest in obscure diseases of the brain and mind.

Graham had resigned his commission before he left India, but he first took steps to secure the property left him by his deceased brother. For this purpose he procured an escort of Sikh horsemen, and, accompanied by them and by a Calcutta lawyer whom he brought up for the purpose, he repaired to his late brother's estate in Central India.

It was a magnificent property; though, as he expected, rumour had exaggerated the amount of wealth accumulated there. At this stage of my story, it will not do to detain the reader by a long description of the estate and the establishment kept up by his deceased relative. The dwelling-house or castle—for it was very strongly fortified, and built in such a way as to resist effectually the efforts of any Asiatic power—was situated on a plateau surrounded by gardens, laid out with the most exquisite taste and skill, and at an enormous expenditure. The apartments of the palace were most magnificent: all the arrangements, fittings, furniture, &c., as well as the architectural style in which it was built, were

Asiatic and Mahometan. Graham sighed, as he walked through the now deserted halls, to think of the moral degradation into which one so nearly related to himself must have sunk to value and appreciate such a mode of life as it was evident he had indulged in. The greater part of the palace was allotted to the harem, in which an immense number of women were living in all the luxurious indolence of the seraglio of an Eastern potentate. The fair inmates—and fair, indeed, they were according to report, for Graham saw nothing of them—had been brought from many different countries. There were Circassians there, purchased in the Turkish slave-markets. There were beauties from Cashmere, Afghanistan, Persia, and India, all congregated to minister to the sensual indulgence of their common lord. Terrible were the wailings and lamentations that arose from that motley throng of bereaved beauties when they heard the mournful news of their lord's decease. Graham had no easy task to settle the accounts of such a household. The property had to be sold, and all these ladies provided with suitable pensions. Those who wished to return to their native land had to be provided with the means of making the journey comfortably, and in a style suitable to their rank in life. The amount of treasure accumulated in the shape of jewels and coin had been, as I said, exaggerated; but still it was very large, and after all the expenses of the settlement had been paid, and the lawyers and agents had received their fees, Graham still found himself in possession of sufficient property to enable him to live comfortably in England.

Why lengthen out my tale? Graham conceived a sudden affection for Lulworth Cove and its neighbourhood. He purchased an estate there, with a fine old mansion on the grounds, whither a short time after he led his young and blooming bride. His father took up his abode with them for the remainder of his days, and there Amy and her husband lived as happily and comfortably ever after as any hero and heroine of a novel are supposed to do.

Brigadier Littlesole no sooner heard of the success that attended the efforts of the party that accompanied Graham and Bowlemover, than he wrote a despatch, describing in detail how application had been made to him for aid, and how he had despatched immediately a party of volunteers, accompanied by a few regular soldiers, to the succour of the survivors at Islamabad, and how all his measures (in organising which his brigade-major, Major

Trumps, had exerted himself in a most praiseworthy manner) had been crowned with the most complete success. Brigadier Littlesole, for these eminent services, was promoted to major-general, and promised the first vacant division, made a K.C.B. and A.D.C. to the Queen, while Major Trumps was made C.B.

There are only two more of my characters about whose fate the reader will feel any concern. They are Miss Trinchinopoly and Dr. Mactartan. Like many others whose adventures have been detailed in the foregoing pages, they, too, returned home after the restoration of tranquillity in India. They returned, but not together. I am sorry to say, Dr. Mactartan, by his conduct, fully justified the evil surmises that had been made about him. During the long time the whole party of fugitives were shut up together in the besieged house and in the tomb, he was constantly thrown into Miss Trinchinopoly's society, more especially as that lady devoted herself to the good work of nursing the sick and wounded who were Dr. Mactartan's especial charge—whether by accident or design who shall say? Their friendship ripened into intimacy, their intimacy into a more tender feeling. They were engaged; and, of course, as her affianced husband, Miss Trinchinopoly entrusted the doctor with the history of her birth and parentage. Alas for human nature! My pen will scarce record the act of black-hearted villany! No sooner had the doctor become possessed of the desired secret, than he grew cool about his engagement, and, to make a long story short, signified his intention of breaking it off.

The lady whose affections had thus been trifled with said nothing, but followed the doctor to Scotland, and, immediately on her arrival, prosecuted him for breach of promise of marriage.

What the mysterious history confided to the ear of her treacherous lover was, has never been divulged, for reasons which will be immediately stated. That it was of importance may be inferred from the fact, that the plaintiff's counsel had instructions, in case defendant adopted a certain line of defence, viz. pleading the history of plaintiff's birth and parentage as a reason for breaking off the match, to throw up the case, and settle it anyhow by arbitration. Defendant's counsel were, of course, ignorant of this; but, contrary to the expectation of the opposite party, they did not adopt this line of defence. Having no other possible excuse to plead, the case, of course, went against defendant, who was cast with damages £700, besides costs to pay.

Poor Dr. Mactartan's savings while in the service were all spent in meeting the heavy expenses of the trial and its consequences, and in this case he paid very dear for his curiosity. He was sitting in his lodgings at Edinburgh one evening, a day or two after the trial, meditating, with the assistance of a pipe and a glass of whisky-toddy, on his future plans, which were considerably affected by the diminution in his worldly means lately caused by his misadventure, when a letter was brought in to him. It proved to be from Miss Trinchinopoly's lawyers, enclosing another from that lady herself. The former contained Dr. Mactartan's cheque for £700 returned to him; the latter informed him that Miss Trinchinopoly had conceived so high an opinion of the doctor's honourable feeling in not having availed himself of the information he had acquired to obtain a more favourable verdict, that she begged to return the amount awarded as 'damages.'

'Faix, but she's a bonny lass!' soliloquised the doctor, after he had read the missives; 'she deserves to be Mrs. Mactartan after all.'

The doctor thought over the subject all that night, and next morning wrote to thank

Miss Trinchinopoly for her liberality and just appreciation of his merits: he concluded by saying, that he had entertained so high an opinion of her character from this little incident—an accident unique in its kind, he was quite sure, in his native country—that if she would consent to let 'bygones be bygones,' and accept his hand, with the £700 in it, he would be only too happy to make it hers, while the secret, being confined to their own bosoms, would be the less likely to become the property of any third person after they had become one.' And so Miss Trinchinopoly became Mrs. Mactartan, and the mystery that hung over the history of her early years was never divulged.

Murray followed Graham's example and resigned his commission. His services were not recognised. A new 19th 'Irregulars' was raised, and the command given to an officer of the royal army who had never seen a shot fired in the field. He did not, however, abandon the profession to which he was so devotedly attached. At first on Garibaldi's staff, and subsequently in command of a brigade under that distinguished man, he was rapidly rising to eminence, when the fate of Italy having been for the time decided, he and his brother-soldiers of fortune had to sheathe their swords.

His talents, however, were appreciated there, and his services did not pass without a reward. He is far from being laid on the shelf, and a marshal's baton of the future Empire of Italy may yet be in store for the quondam commandant of the 19th irregulars.

The bell is ringing, and the curtain must fall. By the right which a magician claims of banishing into thin air the creatures his art has conjured up for the amusement of his audience as soon as they have played their parts upon the stage—so by a wave of my magic wand I bid all the characters of this story—*Presto*—begone! Let the curtain fall. The melodrama is played out. Away with you, soldiers and statesmen, cowards and heroes, wise men and zanies, nawabs, princesses, conspirators, executioners, with all the tragi-comic scenery, palaces and tombs, fortresses and dwelling-houses, drums and cannon, horses and horsemen, banners, and all the paraphernalia of war! Would that I could as easily dismiss from the memory of many a wounded heart the reality which is the counterpart of the melodrama! My tale has been no romance. There is much more of truth than fiction in these pages. Free from personal satire, they contain no highly-coloured or exaggerated representation of real events. The tragic only has been softened down; the lighter element, with its comedy of errors, mistakes, and absurdities, which make one laugh in the midst of horror, is but a bare approximation to the truth. It only remains for me to take leave of my readers who have accompanied me thus far, and assure them my labours will not have been in vain if, while I have enabled them to pass pleasantly a leisure hour, I have shown my countrymen, when they want to hatch rebellion in India and get rid of the country,—HOW TO MANAGE IT.

THE END.

CPSIA information can be obtained
at www.ICGtesting.com
Printed in the USA
LVHW040025180422
716440LV00005B/431

9 783752 594041